BUTTERFLY

A DARK COLLEGE HOCKEY ROMANCE

TABB U
BOOK 1

JO BRENNER

HIGH RISE PUBLISHING

This is a work of fiction. Names, characters, places, and incidents are the product of the author's imagination or are used fictitiously, and any resemblance to actual persons, living or dead, business establishments, events, or locales is entirely incidental.

Editing provided by Surey Rodriguez-Cortes.

Cover design provided by Notorious Cover Design.

Created with Vellum

For everyone who ever fantasized about having a sexy, jealous, and over-the-top possessive stepbrother...

...and then calling him daddy...

Don't worry. Mason's waiting.

ALSO BY JO BRENNER

Bad Heroes

You Can Follow Me

Lose Me In The Shadows

Meet Me In The Dark

NEWSLETTER AND BONUS EPILOGUE

Want to read the bonus epilogue? Join my newsletter for the epilogue, updates, and other goodies! **Click the link below to join and read the bonus epilogue.**

Download Here

BUTTERFLY PLAYLIST

i hate u, i love u
gnash
Bully
Jay.f.k beats
i hope ur miserable until ur dead
Nessa Barrett
WYD Now?
Sadie Jean
Cowbows and Angels
Jessie Murph
Beautiful Things
Benson Boone
I Think He Knows
Taylor Swift
You Need To Calm Down
Taylor Swift
Shameless
Camila Cabello
dirty dishes
KiNG MALA

Don't Blame Me
Taylor Swift
Always Been You
Jessie Murph
I Wouldn't Love Me
Sam Short
MASOCHIST
Thomas Day
Delicate
Taylor Swift

AUTHOR'S NOTE

This one was just really fucking fun to write.

I'm not really sure what else to say here? I was sick with Covid, convalescing in bed, and my brain hurt too much to work on *Meet Me In The Dark*, or a million other things I should have been doing.

For a while I'd been joking with some friends about writing a novella called *My Stepbrother Daddy*. The idea entertained the fuck out of me—and kind of turned me on, to be honest—but I didn't think I'd actually get around to it.

Until there I was in bed, sick, gross, too brain dead to write what I was supposed to write but too bored to do anything else, and I decided...what the hell?

And this story just flowed out of me. I mean, I wrote the first (terrible!) draft in a weekend. And then started posting it to Kindle Vella, because—why not? (That version is still up, by the way, in case you want to compare them.)

It's been through quite a few revisions since then, but as Jo Brenner stories go, it's fairly straightforward. Unlike *Bad Heroes, Butterfly* isn't about trauma, or identity, or how to stop being so fucking afraid of belonging. It *is* a little bit about grief, and how sometimes our perfect puzzle piece is the person whose grief and growth reflects are own...

...so I guess it's a little serious.

But mainly I wanted to write about a hot AF, spoiled AF, emotionally wounded college student who finds out the girl of his dreams is his stepsister—and decides, *fuck it, she's mine anyway.* And how that girl of his dreams is sweet and kind and determined, but needs to learn how to stand up for herself—and battling out with her bully of a stepbrother does just that. I also wanted to write a sex in the stacks scene, and a sex in the locker room scene, and here was the *perfect motherfucking excuse.*

What can I say? Sometimes I miss college.

Again, this is dark, and has a lot of dark shit on it, so please read the content notes on my website, jobrenner.com! As always, my job is to entertain, not to harm...but I need your help in doing so, so please check the warning label before proceeding.

Thank you! Enjoy! No cliffhangers this time, I promise.

Love,

Jo

CONTENT NOTE! PLEASE READ

This is a dark, bully romance, with dark themes and plot points that may be sensitive to some. Please, please, *please* read the content warnings on my website, jobrenner.com. I'd add them here, but the River Platform (IYKYK) could get big mad if it sees the list, and then bye bye, book.

Joking aside, please do visit my website. Your health—mental, physical, spiritual, emotional—matters.

PROLOGUE

MASON

She was the most beautiful girl I'd seen in my entire life.

And I wanted her more than I wanted anything.

I watched as she spun around and around in another man's arms, laughing on the dance floor at my father's wedding. She was tiny and delicate, a pale, black-haired butterfly in a blue dress with hair like satin and skin like silk. And as my eyes followed her, I almost lost my footing—like the earth had tilted off its axis and even gravity had been thrown into chaos.

At eighteen, I'd already been with dozens of girls around my age, and a handful of older women, too. All gorgeous, all sexy, all eager to please. All entertaining until I came, and then immediately forgotten. Honestly, I was fucking bored with all of them. It didn't bode well for my future. But this little slip of a thing caught my attention and held it like no one ever had. And even though I was only eighteen, I already knew no one would ever captivate me the way she did.

I wanted her.

I would have her.

Ignoring the fairy lights hanging from the trellis, the candles and flowers surrounding the pool at our family home, and the laughing, chattering guests, I focused on the guy she was with. Some young, skinny jackass who clearly didn't realize what a loser he was, or how undeserving he was of the perfection in his arms. It wouldn't take much to scare him off.

I was on my way to do so, and to get my hands on her tight, sweet, supple body, when a hand fell onto my shoulder and gripped hard.

"Mason," my father said.

"Paul." I'd stopped calling him Dad a long time ago. He'd stopped *being* a dad after Mom had died five years ago and he'd abandoned me to his grief. And here he was, abandoning me again for some gold-digger he'd found and fallen for.

Well, fuck him.

Paul coughed. He hated when I called him by his first name.

"I'd like you to spend some time getting to know your new stepmother and stepsister. Anna's still mingling with guests, but I'd like us to spend the rest of the summer together. And I see that you've spotted your stepsister, Leslie."

My whole body went cold. I ripped my eyes off the butterfly in blue to turn and look at him. "What do you mean?"

He nodded toward the dance floor, face grim. "That's your new stepsister."

This time, I did stumble.

Stepsister.

My fantasy of introducing myself to her, seducing her,

and seeing what her body looked like underneath that blue dress disappeared quickly as reality intruded. She was my stepsister. Not only could I not have her—*never* have her—she was the daughter of the woman I hated, the woman who was trying to replace my dead mother. I wanted nothing to do with this new family my father was assembling in an attempt to forget the love of his life who had given him everything.

My mother had been everything to me, until the car accident. Then she'd just been...gone. And my father acted like he'd forgotten.

I shoved those thoughts aside, continuing to watch her, my stepsister, the lust and awe burning into ash.

"Listen, Mason. I know I'm not your favorite person, and you're angry at me for remarrying, but I'm telling you—treat our new family right, or I'll make sure you regret it." He squeezed my shoulder again, and I tried not to flinch. "You hear me?"

"I hear you," I said through gritted teeth.

"Good." He lifted a hand to his mouth. "Leslie, come join us."

The butterfly paused, saying something to her partner. He kissed her—a light peck, but seeing his lips against hers made me want to break something.

I couldn't help but stare at her bare legs as she made her way toward us. Even walking, she looked like she was dancing.

When she reached us, she stared up at me, her dark eyes soft and curious.

The ground threatened to start spinning again.

I ignored it—and the pain in my chest at knowing this perfect creature wouldn't be mine. I'd always been good at projecting guilt and externalizing blame—I'd learned it from my father, after all. So it didn't take much to shift my frustration at the universe into anger at *her*. This was her fault. She didn't have to be so innocently seductive, such a forbidden temptation.

Was it a little crazy to blame my new stepsister for wanting her? Sure. But it would save me.

"Leslie," my father greeted her warmly, wrapping an arm around her and kissing her on the cheek. And even though I knew his affection toward her was nothing more than fatherly, I wanted to rip him away from her.

"Hi Paul," she said fondly. Her voice was high and clear, wrapping around me with a sweetness that stabbed at my chest.

"Leslie, I'd like you to meet someone. This is Mason, my son."

She tilted her head back to look up at me. Her face was warm and friendly. "I guess that makes you my stepbrother, doesn't it!"

I caught myself licking my lips as I stared at hers, pink and full and begging for my cock. Instead, I laughed bitterly. "I see you get your intelligence from your mother."

She reared back, offended. "Excuse me, what did you just say to me?"

"Mason," my father warned.

I shrugged, showing her my teeth. "Sorry."

Glaring, she shrugged, mirroring me. "Apology not accepted."

I laughed despite myself. An aggressive butterfly, then.

Before she could snap at me again, Anna, her mother, appeared next to us. My father put his arm around the buxom blonde as well.

Leslie must take after her father, whatever had happened to him.

"Oh, I see you two have met!" Anna trilled happily. "I'm so glad. Mason, Leslie just graduated from The Brooklyn School of the Arts. Leslie, Mason is about to start his freshman year at Harvard. But you'll both be home this summer, so Mason, I hope you can show her around town and give her the lay of the land."

"Oh, I can give her the lay of the land, all right," I said smoothly.

Leslie's cheeks turned pink. "Mom, I thought we talked about this. I don't want to spend the summer in Westchester. Bea said I could stay with her and her parents in Harlem. I'll be closer to the dance studio that way..."

"Leslie! You spend all year with Bea, completely focused on dance. Don't you want to spend some time with your family? Don't you miss me?" her mom wheedled.

So she was a dancer. That explained the toned thighs, perfect posture, and ethereal way she moved.

It didn't explain my desperate need to rip that dress off her and get my mouth between those toned thighs.

It wasn't going to happen.

I wanted her gone, before I did something that we'd both regret.

"Excuse me," I said. "But I need to be somewhere right now."

"But we haven't even gotten to the toasts yet!" Anna protested.

My father stared at me.

I nodded my head toward Tiffanie, my on-again, off-again girlfriend I'd forgotten on the side of the dance floor the moment I'd seen Leslie dancing. She was glaring at us, mouth pinched in a frown.

"I've been a bad boyfriend and left my date alone. She deserves some of my time, no?"

Anna relaxed, smiling. "Oh, that's nice. Young love," she trilled. "Maybe you can double-date with Leslie and her boyfriend, Spencer."

There was no way in hell I'd be doing that.

From the expression on Leslie's face, she felt the same way.

"Nice to meet you, Lily," I said.

She raised an eyebrow. "Nice to meet you too, Jason," she retorted, and as I walked away, I couldn't help but smile at her attempt at a power play.

But my smile dropped off my face as I remembered that was the only time we'd ever be playing.

I grabbed Tiffanie by her arm and dragged her off with me without saying anything.

"Where have you been?" she asked in what I'd always thought was a sexy voice until now.

I had a growing fear I'd never think a single voice was sexy if it wasn't high and clear and sounded like bells over water.

I didn't bother to answer her. "I need you to suck my cock."

"Of course, baby," she said.

I dragged her into the pool house, ignoring the other guests, the sound of metal on glass as the toasts began. I ignored everything as Tiffanie got on her knees, unzipped my pants, and pulled my hard cock out.

"You were that excited thinking about me, weren't you, baby?" she crooned, and I didn't bother to correct her.

I wasn't hard for her.

I was hard for a butterfly who would remain just outside of my grasp, unless I set fire to her wings.

As Tiffanie's mouth worked my cock, I fisted her hair, trying to focus. Usually her blonde, carefully-constructed waves and huge tits did it for me, but not tonight. I didn't want blonde curls and curves, I wanted straight black hair and a lithe, petite body. So I imagined Leslie in front of me instead, her dark hair falling around her shoulders as her pert mouth gave me pleasure. I imagined coming down her tight little throat, on her tiny, perky tits, or on her perfect, beautiful face.

Pleasure rushed through me at the thought, followed by anger.

Some people pinned butterflies to keep them close.

I was going to make this one fly far, far away.

After all, she was the most beautiful girl I'd seen in my entire life.

I wanted her more than I wanted anything.

And I hated her for it.

1

LESLIE

I fucking hated the motherfucker.

You know that feeling? When hating someone fuels you with so much spite it makes you feel alive? That's how I felt about my goddamned stepbrother.

Mason Calloway. Or "Ohmygod, Maaaaaace!" according to all the girls who sighed and giggled when he drove by them in his Tesla or hung out at his pool in tiny bikinis, hoping that he'd wife them up.

Spoiler alert, he never did. Even his girlfriend, Tiffanie, was only there to ride his dick.

I'd been excited to meet my new stepbrother at first, until he'd insulted me and my mother to my face—in front of my new stepdad. My mom had been through enough in life. After we learned that we were my father's side family—and he left to go be with his real family without looking back—she swore off men. To me, it had felt like she also swore off happiness. So I was ecstatic that she'd finally found a man who treated her like she was the sun itself. No one mistreated her, especially not some silver spoon-fed, pompous asshole who happened to be so incredibly gorgeous it almost hurt to look at him.

Mason was tall, and built, and his muscles needed their own zip code. That night, the fairy lights around his father's pool had lit his tan and sparkled in his blue eyes, so dark they were almost navy. Freckles scattered across his cheeks, making him almost pretty. Pale blond hair fell in waves over his eyes. He had the beauty of wealth, privilege, and never having to worry about anything in life.

Yeah, I hated him.

Even if there'd been a moment there, when his eyes were on mine and he'd licked his lips, when desire and an unfamiliar longing had shot through me.

And then he'd opened that gorgeous, cruel mouth and ruined it all.

I see you get your intelligence from your mother.

Yeah, fuck that asshole. And not in a (I imagined; I was a virgin after all) fun way.

After that insulting interaction, Mason had full-out ignored me, turning to talk to someone else every time I addressed him, as if I didn't exist—or wasn't worthy of his attention.

I had just barely resisted screaming in his beautiful face or throwing wedding cake at his stupid head. I wanted his attention, and his apology, and it was driving me Up. The. Wall. First, because I didn't need some asshole's time or energy. And second, he was my *stepbrother*, and so whatever desire I felt toward him was completely wrong, no matter how sexy I unfortunately found his arrogance to be.

After the wedding, my stepfather took my mom away on their mini-moon.

"I'll go back to Bea's then, in the city," I told my mom the next morning after the wedding.

We stood in the unfamiliar, massive, metal and marble kitchen, and I tried to adjust to seeing my mom in there. It was her kitchen now, and she seemed happy in it, so I was determined to be happy for her.

"Oh honey, that's unnecessary. Just stay here," my mom wheedled, pouting at me. It was her superpower, so I relented. Even when she added, "Mason can keep you company, can't you, sweetheart?"

Mason lifted an eyebrow in response. My mom's cheeks colored in the embarrassment of his silent rejection.

That's it, I'd had enough. If I had to spend time with this asshole to make her happy, I would.

"We'll be fine, Mom," I told her, smiling. The moment she looked away, I turned my head to my new stepbrother and glared.

Be nice, I mouthed.

A smirk spread across his mouth as he shook his head slowly.

Oh my god, this motherfucking asshole. No one this douchey should be this attractive.

But I wasn't going to tell on him, not when Paul was already rolling their bags to the door to meet their driver (because my mom had a *driver* now). He glanced at his son, and although I didn't understand his look, I could tell it was meaningful, especially when a vein in Mason's neck popped.

And then they were gone, and it was just the two of us in this big, strange house.

Well, the two of us and twenty of his best friends.

It had been a nonstop party since our parents had left. Mason's friends had all been jerks to me, treating me like a maid, or like I was invisible. The girls—who I usually got along with *just fine*—were especially rude. I had no idea what I'd done, but I was getting sick of it. To top it off, the house stank of weed and alcohol, and at night, Mason and his friends disappeared into the pool house, the music so loud I couldn't sleep.

I tossed and turned in bed for hours, even resorting to using my airpods to drown out the noise, but they were really uncomfortable to sleep in. Finally, I gave up, stuffing my feet into flip flops and going down to the pool house to confront him.

I pushed the door open. The pool house was filled with smoke, writhing bodies, and the thudding rhythm of club versions of pop songs. Mason was absolutely nowhere to be found. Instead, his friend Emory leaned in the doorway, smirking at me as he inhaled a spliff, green eyes red and glassy. He was shorter than Mason, although buffer, with thick brown hair that probably tempted most girls to touch it. But not me. I felt nothing for Emory but aggravation.

"The stepsister," he greeted me, eyeing me up and down with a leer. "To what do we owe the pleasure?"

I didn't have time for this. Sure, I was in booty shorts and a sports bra—it was what I slept in, usually—but the girls around him were in bikinis; I was dressed like a nun in comparison.

"Where's Mason?"

"Busy. Tell me, stepsister, are you a prude? Or do you get off on the ice princess vibe?"

I reared back, shocked. *Ice princess.* I was nothing of the sort. I just didn't want anything to do with my stepbrother's friends.

"Sorry, I guess I have a hard time being *warm* and *friendly* when I'm this short on sleep. I bet if you all turned the music down, and I could get the necessary seven to eight hours, I'd be much sweeter." To emphasize this, I flashed him an insincere smile, glaring daggers at the same time.

Emory laughed. "You've got fire. I like that. Mason's over there. But he's, well..." he coughed. "Busy. As I'm sure you can see."

He stepped out of the way. Back against the wall, I spotted my douche of a stepbrother. And when I saw what he was up to, my stomach dropped to my feet for reasons I didn't want to investigate.

His girlfriend, Tiffanie, the bitchiest of the bunch, was leaning against his left shoulder and kissing him—sloppy and drunk.

And between his legs was one of her friends, bobbing her head, my stepbrother's dick in her mouth.

I rolled my eyes. I refused to be annoyed. After all, if Tiffanie was okay with some other girl blowing her boyfriend, that was her prerogative.

So then why did it feel like someone had punched me in the chest?

As if he could feel my eyes on him, Mason opened his eyes, staring straight at me as Tiffanie continued to play tonsil tennis with him. His eyes were the cold blue of the Artic Ocean, and just as hard. They didn't move off mine as he lifted his hips and thrust into the other girl's mouth.

My face burned. Scratch that, everything burned. It was like my whole body had been doused in gasoline and lit on fire.

Behind me, Emory choked on a laugh. "Like I said, he's busy."

At that moment, I had two options. I could run out of there like a bat out of a hell, and avoid the fuck out of Mason and his friends until our parents got back in a few days. Part of me wanted to do that. I was embarrassed, and I wasn't sure why. I hadn't done anything wrong.

Exactly. I hadn't done anything wrong. Which brought me to my second option: Stay. Stay, and prove that I was unphased, to Mason...and to myself. Stay, and show my *darling, dearest stepbrother Mace* that I wasn't the delicate flower he thought I was. I wasn't a coward, and he couldn't scare me.

You want to make him jealous, a voice in my head pointed out.

I ignored it. Why the hell would I want to make my stepbrother jealous?

And yet my actions mimicked a jealous woman's. I reached for Emory's hand and tugged him behind me as I made my way to the makeshift dance floor, intent on remaining directly in Mason's line of sight. With a surprised grunt, Emory followed me, staring at me in alarm when I turned and faced him and began moving my hips to the music. I was careful not to look at Mason, but I didn't need to—I could feel his dark eyes burning into me, further fanning the flames.

It was like I was two people. One was watching in shock, aware of my stepbrother's—what? Disapproval?—and confused by and worried about my choices and what they might mean. The other part of me got lost in the music and the heat of my stepbrother's gaze, letting my body take over as I took Emory's hands in mine and lowered them to my hips.

"I don't think—" he began.

"So don't think," I retorted, moving against him.

I'd been dancing since I could walk, and even though ballet was my style of choice, I knew how to twist and roll and pop my body in ways that caught men's attention. I wasn't much to look at, the very definition of a plain Jane. But I could dance.

"Fuck, I'm so screwed," Emory muttered, proving me right. He gave in and began to dance with me, tugging me closer so I could feel his hardening dick against my stomach. Usually this was something that would make me recoil —I had Spencer, after all, my on-and-off-again boyfriend, even if we were more off than on these days—but I forced myself to relax, wrapping my arms around Emory's neck and focusing on his chest in front of me.

I felt nothing, of course, except for satisfaction.

As the song slowed to something sexy and sultry, I whipped around and bumped my ass against Emory's dick, then dropped low and rolled back up, grinding against him.

There was a loud growl, a feminine, high-pitched, "What the hell?!" and then Mason was in front of me, zipping up his pants. I glanced down; he was still hard. He also was breathing like he was a bull and Emory's and my writhing bodies were red flags.

Emory must have sensed it too, because he stepped away from me.

"Look, man..." he began.

Mason interrupted him. "I'll deal with you later."

"Problem, stepbrother dearest?" I trilled.

"You know there is. You aren't welcome here." His eyes were no longer that icy blue. Instead, they were dark and heated, lit by the same flames that lit me. My pulse raced. I was both triumphant—and terrified. I'd won something, some game between us, but I didn't know what that game was, and I was one hundred percent positive I didn't want to find out.

"It's my home, too. No one told me the pool house is off

limits. Besides, it's a party, isn't it? I just want to dance," I said.

"You weren't invited. So get out."

Ouch, that fucking stung.

"Hey man, she's just dancing. Maybe let's call a truce," Emory interjected, trying to bring peace to the war that was clearly coming.

"Yeah? I'm sure Paul and my mom would *love* to hear about your exclusive parties in their home. And how receptive and welcoming you've been," I said.

"Leslie, you do *not* want to fuck with me," Mason warned.

The thing was, I *did*. This wasn't like me—I was too smart to go up against an opponent who was, by all evidence, likely to destroy me. Hell, I'd never *had* an opponent before Mason. Not even in ballet, which was known for being cutthroat and competitive. My teachers used to joke that, in addition to having excellent feet, I had major peacekeeping abilities that made even the meanest of the other ballerinas in our youth company want to be my friends. It wasn't that there wasn't drama at my ballet school, but it never involved me, and I was never the mean girls' target.

So then what the hell was going on now? How had I ended up in this situation?

And god, why did I *like* it?

"Maybe I do," I said, breathless. If I hadn't already lost my breath, I would've at the look in his eyes—intense and, if I wasn't wrong, lustful.

He moved deeper into my space, wrapping a hand in my hair and pulling it back, and back, and back, so even though he was so much taller than me, I stared straight at him.

"Careful, butterfly. Or I'll really think you want to play with me."

There was a promise in his eyes, and I considered testing it, discovering what it was.

Fortunately, rational Leslie woke up and screamed at me to get the hell out of there. Take option one, like I should have earlier.

So I did, running out the door, the sound of people's laughter following—as well as Mason's inexplicable growl.

2

LESLIE

It didn't take long for Mason's games to begin.

They were tiny things at first: My contact solution going missing, then my car keys. The music was even louder the following night, but I didn't bother going back down there to tell him to turn it down. Instead, I threw myself into dance, finding a studio within easy driving distance and signing up for classes. Dance was my version of self-care, even as it slowly destroyed my body. The blisters, the bruised toes and broken toenails, the physical strain and exhaustion—it was all worth it, for those moments when I lost myself in the music and became someone else: strong, powerful, beautiful. I loved that version of me.

Which was why I was so angry that morning.

I had a pointe class, my first since the wedding and the move. It seemed like a good way to get out of the house until our parents got home the next day. I did *not* want to be late to ballet. Instructors were notorious for holding grudges, especially regarding tardiness. And even though I was only going to be in Westchester for a few months, I wanted to make a good first impression. My reputation meant everything to me, and so did the approval of authority figures. Daddy issues, and all that.

I rolled my eyes at my thoughts as I bent down to pick up my pointe shoes from the corner of the room, only to immediately drop them.

They were soaking wet.

And slimy.

And covered in a white, viscous liquid that—I picked one up between my forefinger and thumb and carefully, warily, took a sniff—yup, smelled like sour sex.

My lungs went tight.

It was semen.

Mason—or one of his friends, but something about it made me sure it was Mason—had jacked off on my pointe shoes.

Who did something like that?!

I slammed out of my room, carefully holding the shoes in their only dry spot, ready to confront the nasty motherfucker and throw them at his head.

Only to slam to stop.

Sure, I could yell at him, but what good would that do? He'd only know he'd gotten to me.

No, I needed to get even. That motherfucker had destroyed something I loved. It was time I did the same to him.

I tossed the toe shoes in the trash, then grabbed my backup pair from the closet, checking my phone. If I hurried, I'd make it.

And then, after class, I was going to make a trip to the grocery store before returning to home *sweet* home.

"What the fuck is this?"

Mason's usually icy, level voice rose to a low roar as he slapped a noxious smelling object down on the kitchen counter.

"I think that's a dead fish," I told him helpfully as I continued to chop a cucumber.

He roared again. "I know that much, Leslie. What I want to know is *what the hell was it doing in my car?*"

"You know, Elon Musk is a real dirtbag," I told him, popping a slice of cucumber into my mouth and pretending to be unaffected by the stench.

"That's my *car*," he repeated. "I don't know if I'm ever going to be able to get the smell out."

I shrugged. "You want me to leave your shit alone, leave my shit alone."

The coldness in his eyes receded, only leaving amusement. "Ah, you saw my...present, did you?"

I glared at him, then looked down. I was brandishing the chef's knife at him.

Oops. "I wouldn't call that filth a 'present.'"

He smirked. "Funny, most girls would say differently."

"Then maybe you should come on *their* shoes."

"Oh, butterfly," he tsked, crowding me, apparently uncaring that the point of the knife was pushing up against his sternum. "Before we're done, you'll be *begging* for my come—everywhere."

"Why the fuck would you say something like that?" I choked out. "Seriously, Mason. That's fucked."

His eyes flashed. He glared down at the knife, and then

backed away, until he leaned against the fridge, arms crossed, as he transferred the glare to me.

The look on his face confused me. He didn't seem like the type to back away from a fight. So why had he? And why did he seem so much angrier about what I'd said than he had about the fish?

"I'll tell you what's fucked," he began. "It's having to entertain and look after a goddamned fragile little interloper—"

"—Who the fuck are you calling fragile—" I interjected.

He ignored me, continuing. "—who has no business being in my home when all I want to do is drag her to the ground and—"

Drag me to the ground? My lungs seized at the image in my head, on the floor, his large body on top of mine, his mouth swallowing me up, so wrong, but so good, and—

"Hellloooooooo!" The front door slammed open as my mother trilled the greeting from the front door.

"Hey kids," Paul called.

Oh.

Oh fuck.

What had I been fucking thinking?

I stared at Mason, who stared back.

"Stay away from me," I hissed. "And don't say *anything.*"

"What, butterfly," he said, and I wanted to smack that smirk off his face. "Scared that if they know how we're 'getting along' it'll ruin the little fantasy life your gold-digger mother has created for the two of you?"

"Call. Her. That. One. More. Time. And I will slice that smirk off your face," I said, threatening him with the chef's knife I still held in my hand.

Something lit in his blue eyes. "Not fragile, then. Feisty."

"You don't even know, *Mace.* You have no fucking idea how feisty I can be."

The truth was, *I* also didn't know how feisty I could be. I wasn't usually like this. I was sweet, and calm, and I liked myself that way, even if I wish I was better at standing up for myself. My stepbrother had found some darker part of my soul, and I wasn't sure how I felt about it.

With that, he pushed off the fridge and wandered up the stairs, ignoring my mother when she called out a hello.

"Mason," his father called.

"Going to the rink," Mason said. "Need ice time."

Ice time? My stepbrother was a hockey player? As much as I hated him, I found a little bit of respect for him—he wasn't just some spoiled rich boy, he had to have some amount of determination and drive to be an athlete, after all. I should've realized as much based on his physique, but then I was hit with images of Mason in his skates and nothing else—

"What's gotten into him?" my mother asked, perturbed. She'd be even more perturbed if she realized where my head had gone. She opened her arms to hug me, then froze, wrinkling her nose in disgust. "And why is there a branzino on the kitchen counter? Honey, I hope you weren't planning on making that. It smells off."

I bit my lips to keep from giggling. Or screaming. I wasn't sure which; Mason made me feel so many things.

Too many things.

All the things.

I really fucking hated it, as much, if not more, than I hated him.

Paul watched me, his blue eyes—so much like his son's—working. It worried me, what he was figuring out. Would he kick me out if he knew I'd put a dead fish in the car he'd bought his son? Would he kick his *son* out, if he knew what Mason had done to my toe shoes? I shouldn't care what happened to Mason, but part of me did—the same part who had stared at him with longing that first moment when we'd met. Plus, I didn't know what that kind of family fracture would do to his relationship with my mom, and her happiness.

"Yeah," I murmured. "I was just planning on tossing it. Maybe we can get pizza?"

3

LESLIE

After that, things went from bad to worse. Two days later, I showed up at the dance studio to giggles and weird looks from the two girls at the front desk.

"Um, Leslie..." one said, before bursting in laughter again.

My stomach sank. "What's wrong?"

The other held out a pair of underwear.

My underwear.

"We received a package of a number of these yesterday, with a note."

Rage made my body go stiff and still. I didn't have to look in a mirror to see how red my face was. I also didn't need to see the note to know who the culprit was, but when the woman handed it over to me, I took it.

With shaking fingers, I opened the folded, embossed note with the initials MC.

THESE ARE FOR LESLIE BERGER, SO IF SHE HAS AN "ACCIDENT," SHE HAS EXTRAS.

SHE'S PRONE TO THEM.
THANKS,
MASON

"Wow, Mason Calloway must really hate you," the other girl remarked, tossing her hair. "What did you do to him?"

"He's my stepbrother," I said through gritted teeth. "And I'm going to kill him."

The first girl shrugged. "I wouldn't take Mason on, if I were you. They don't call him Ice Man for nothing—and it's not just because he's an *incredible* center."

"He'll destroy you, Leslie. Take the L," the other girl advised.

But even though there was some sympathy in her voice, neither of them were on my side. No, they weren't going to go up against the titan of their little wealthy town. I was on my own—and I'd never felt more alienated in my life.

I texted Bea.

he's still fucking with me

what did he do this time?

mailed all my underwear to the dance studio

There was a pause as she digested this. Then:

wow, that asshole is not playing around.
What are you going to do?

hit him back where it hurts

hard

I was determined to win this fight. Bea, though, had some qualms.

> les, are you sure? maybe you should back down
>
> this isn't going anywhere good
>
> just tell your mom you want to come stay with me

But I knew that would break my mom's heart.

And furthermore, I wasn't about to forfeit. No, if the Ice Man wanted a war, he'd have one.

And I had just the idea for my next battle strategy.

Fortunately, when I got home from the studio, no one was home.

Dropping my bag off in my room, I tiptoed down the Berber-carpeted hallway. Even though I knew I was alone, I was worried I'd get caught. There'd be hell to pay if Mason caught me in his room.

But I'd been dosed with bravery and spite, and I was carrying this mission out.

The door to his bedroom was locked, but I had bobby pins from ballet—and knew how to pick a lock. Prying a bobby pin open, I put my ear to the door and turned it a few times, until I heard the telltale snick and the knob turned.

Aha. Step one, complete.

I pulled the door open, stepping inside my evil step-brother's room. His scent, something spicy, something musky, something sweet, filled my nostrils and over-whelmed me, making me shiver. It was because of the threat the scent represented, *not* because I wanted to roll around in it like a dog.

The room was neat as a pin. Paul had a housekeeper,

which had been weird to get used to, but this was a whole different level. The books were stacked carefully against each other, the bed was made, and there wasn't a single sock on the floor. Nothing like the other teenage boys I knew, like Spencer, who was a complete slob.

There was no art on the walls, and only one photo. In it, a much younger Mason and a beautiful blonde woman smiled at the camera, arms wrapped around each other.

Oh, Mason.

I knew from my mom that he'd lost his mother slowly, painfully, and both Calloway men had been helpless and lost and angry at the world once she was gone. Paul had my mom now—not as a replacement for his beloved wife, but a new love to help staunch that wound.

What did Mason have?

I almost abandoned my plan then and there, but the memory of the dance studio employees' giggles made me square my shoulders. I could feel bad for him, but that didn't mean what he was doing to me was okay. I needed to fight fire with fire.

Opening his closet, I ignored the carefully folded jeans and t-shirts, hockey uniforms, and suits he must wear on game days, spotting a shelf with three pairs of skates, stored upside down with the blades shining on top. A little box on the left held Mason's skate guards.

Bingo.

I'd overheard Emory teasing Mason the other day about his lucky skates, and, well...one of these had to be lucky.

But since I wasn't sure, I guess I'd have to take all of them.

They were being donated to the Yellow Toad, a thrift shop that raised money for homeless youth. Really, Mason should thank me for the service I was doing for him. He didn't need all the luck. He'd be glad he was helping the community.

Although it was more likely he'd kill me.

I couldn't wait to see the look on his face.

4

LESLIE

I woke up from a sweaty, confusing dream that left my sheets wet and me with my heart in my throat.

Someone was in my room. Watching me.

I sensed him there, in a dark corner of my room, looming and threatening. And the threat was physical, but in ways I wasn't ready to accept yet. The dream still clung to me, hot skin against hot skin, sepia tones and the feeling of a very wrong-rightness, not quite ready to release me to consciousness.

"You talk in your sleep," the main character from my dream remarked in a low, husky voice.

Well, now I was wide awake.

I sat straight up in bed, feeling around wildly for some sort of weapon before remembering that I was anti-violence of all kinds.

Even against sexy evil stepbrothers.

"Why are you in my room, Mason?" I asked.

"What did you do with my skates?" he asked, and his quiet tone belied a terrifying menace. This was a man who would hurt me without regret.

Still, I had promised myself I wouldn't back down without a fight.

"Donated them to a good cause. You're welcome," I said, shrugging a shoulder.

Unfortunately, it made my sleep shirt slip down over my shoulder. It was too dark to see Mason's eyes, but I could feel the heat of his stare on my bare skin. The contrast between his attention and the slight chill of the AC made goosebumps break out everywhere, and I shivered.

"No thank you," he spat. "Because not only did you donate all my skates—"

"—Can't you just buy new ones?" I countered, knowing differently.

"One of the pairs were my lucky skates."

Got him.

As scared as I was, it didn't cancel out my satisfaction.

"Well," I said, flipping my hair over my shoulders and hiding my bare flesh from his gaze, "I doubt a man like you needs luck."

He stood and walked a step, then two, toward the bed.

Oh god. Ohgodohgodohgod. My pulse picked up.

As he loomed over me, the dream fought its way back to the surface. He'd crawled on top of me in the dream, held me down, before he—

"You might be right," he acknowledged, approaching from the side and leaning down over me, so I could feel the warmth of his breath on my face. "But princess, I hope you know what you've done."

"Nothing worse than *mailing my underwear to my dance studio*," I said.

"Oh, Leslie, do you really think this is the worst I can do?" his teeth gleamed in the darkness, and I watched, transfixed, as one of his hands descended, tucking a loose strand of hair behind my ear.

Had I shivered before? If that had been a shiver, this was a quake—a seismic shift in my whole body, maybe even my soul.

"I'm not fragile, remember?" I said, my voice breathy, shaking.

"No," he mused, his fingers trailing over my ear. I had to freeze my body to stone to keep from leaning into his touch.

Stepbrother, stepbrother, stepbrother, I chanted to myself silently. *Evil, evil, evil.*

"This means war, butterfly. I hope you're ready."

With that, he released my hair and prowled out the door, closing it quietly behind him.

I collapsed onto the bed, suddenly exhausted.

What had I done?

I GOT PULLED OVER THE NEXT DAY BY COPS, WHO CLAIMED they had a warrant to search my car for drugs—which they *found.* If it weren't for Paul's attorneys—and god, was *that* an embarrassing phone call—I would've spent the night in jail.

When Paul asked how it happened, I told him it was a silly prank from high school friends.

"Some kind of prank," he remarked, his eyes seeing too much. "Leslie, if there's anything you want to tell me—"

But it wasn't only about my mother's happiness, not anymore. Tattling on Mason would be the same thing as forfeiting, and I refused to lose this war. Even though my stepbrother was trying to ruin my life.

Instead, I sent an anonymous email to Harvard saying that he had cheated on his AP exams. They didn't kick him out—they wouldn't, when Paul had made such an extravagant donation—but it was sure to put him on shaky footing when he started there.

I heard them arguing in Paul's office, after. I heard the words "absolute disappointment" and "what would your mother think?"

After, Mason slammed out the door, catching me on the top of the stairs.

He shook his head at me, his face grim—and haunted in a way that almost made me regret what I was doing. But I couldn't stop—and neither could he.

We continued to one up each other throughout the summer, as the tension between us tightened—right under our parents' noses. I would be lying if I said that trying to bring him down didn't take over my entire life. See, having a nemesis is like drinking a vat of coffee on a day you've had no sleep—you feel shaky and tingly all over, like you can conquer the world, but you also want to cry, and time passes by in a blur while you behave without any sense of reality or consequence.

And sometimes it makes you feel more alive than anything ever has.

I didn't know this at the time, however. Or if I did, I denied it to myself. All I knew was that at some point, this had to stop.

I was in the kitchen one morning when I expressed this to him.

"We need to call a truce, Mason."

"Why, butterfly?" he said, smirking. His eyes were turquoise with mockery. "We're having so much fun."

I glared. "If we continue this way, someone's going to get killed. What's your endgame here, anyway? To get me to leave? There's only six more weeks left of summer before we both head off to school—I'd love it if I could have some peace."

He shook his head.

"Not going to happen."

Why did that fill me with a fizzy, buoyant feeling?

"Then I'm telling Paul everything."

He glared, then sighed.

"Fine. Truce."

I stared at him, untrusting.

"You mean that?" I asked.

"Yeah." He shrugged, smiling. "You gave as good as you got, butterfly. I almost respect you for it."

My heart slowed, relief—and something that felt disturbingly like disappointment—filling my chest.

"Truce."

He held out his hand. "Shake on it?"

I put my hand in his, bemused by how his engulfed mine, and beyond freaked out by the tingles his touch sent through me. Was this the first time I'd ever touched him consensually? I tried to push the sense-memory of his fingers stroking my ear out of my mind.

If so, I was never touching him again. This must be what a heart attack felt like.

Unfortunately, he didn't let my hand go, instead holding it captive and turning it to rub circles on my palm with his thumb.

"Mason, what are you doing?" God, my voice sounded breathy.

"I don't know," he admitted, finally releasing me. "But I recommend you stay away from me before things get even more out of hand."

I should've listened to him.

5

LESLIE

It was disturbingly quiet from then on. Mason must have taken our truce to heart and taken the partying elsewhere, but the silence was almost as disruptive as the music had been. A few nights later, unable to sleep, I decided to go for a swim. It was late, almost midnight, and the house was quiet, the pool lit a dark turquoise by the fairy lights that hadn't been taken down after the wedding. My bathing suits were in the wash, but I figured there wasn't any harm in swimming in my panties and bralette, especially if my parents were asleep and Mason was at Tiffanie's.

Just the thought of him with her filled me with an agitation I loathed. I loathed him. He was my stepbrother. Maybe if I said it enough times, I would begin to believe it.

As I swam laps in the warm, dark night, I heard a splash. I stopped swimming, treading water as a shadowy figure approached me. But I recognized the height, the build: Mason was a big guy, lean but tall, made of muscles. His blonde hair was dark from the water as he swam toward me.

"If you try to kill me, I'll get you arrested," I told him,

trying not to show him any fear. "And then poof! There goes Harvard for real this time."

"Big words for the girl trapped in the pool with me this late at night." His eyes glittered in the moonlight, like they'd swallowed the stars.

If I wasn't careful, they'd swallow me up, too.

I backed away.

"I'll scream."

He started to respond, then shook his head, splashing me with droplets of water. "Too easy."

I didn't bother to ask what he meant, just waded over to the edge of the pool, determined to escape him.

"Not so fast, butterfly," he said, swimming up behind me and grabbing me by the waist. His hands—warm and hard and huge—wrapped around my bare midriff, sending tingles through me. Briefly, I wondered what else of his was warm and hard and huge, before shaking the thought away like a swimmer dislodging water from their ears. Nothing good followed that thought, no matter how objectively hot my stepbrother and tormentor was.

"Let me go," I told him, careful to keep my voice steady.

"Maybe I don't want to," he told me, and the words struck me as unbearably honest.

For a moment, neither of us spoke. He tightened his hold on me, and leaned his head into my shoulder, breathing heat into my ear and making me squirm back against him.

And then I had my answer. He was hard, and warm, and felt pretty huge behind me.

"You don't want to do this," I told him. "You hate me, remember?"

He sighed, rotating his hips so his cock rubbed hard against my ass. "That's right, butterfly. I hate you. This here," he jerked against me again, "is hate, pure and simple. Want to hate me back?"

"Mason, if you don't let me go..."

He released me, taking a step back. Suddenly I felt cold all over, and completely confused. My body ached, my thighs trembling, and I... I desperately needed to come.

I hated myself for it.

"Fly off then, butterfly. Go on, I won't chase you." His final words were a dark, terrifying promise. "This time."

I fled.

FOR THE REST OF THE NIGHT, I TOSSED AND TURNED, DREAMS filled with the disturbing heat of Mason's hands all over me. Appalled at myself—not only was he an asshole, not only did I have Spencer, but he was my *stepbrother*—I never fell back asleep, just paced my room and tried to decide what to do. Mason was problematic, but I couldn't lay all the blame on him. Because on some deep, dark, fucked up level, I clearly wanted him.

Holy. Fucking. Hell.

The next morning, he was being obscenely nice—for him. I tiptoed down the stairs to the kitchen, hoping I'd miss him—only to hear the noise coming from the pool.

Great. All of his seven million friends were here. And probably Tiffanie. And *that,* my friends, was jealousy I felt, damn it.

He was my *stepbrother.* I was going to hell.

The sliding door to the pool opened and Mason was there. I did my best to ignore the way water dripped down his chest, pooling at his abs. One droplet continued to slide down to his treasure trail.

Obviously, I'd failed.

He didn't call me out for my ogling, though. Just moved toward the fridge, opening the door and grabbing a bottle of water. He uncapped it, chugging it down, and I once again tried and failed to ignore the way his throat worked, Adam's apple bobbing as he drank.

Finally, he wiped his mouth. "Come outside," he said, voice gruff.

"I don't think that's a good idea."

"Leslie. Come outside."

So, maybe not nice. But more welcoming than he had been before.

After going back upstairs and changing into a bikini, I grabbed a towel and headed outside, hesitantly picking my way through the drunk, laughing, gyrating bodies to a lounger and laying out on it. I waited, chest tight, for Mason to do something fucked up and prove to me I'd been wrong to trust him, but he and his friends just splashed around in the pool. Exhausted from the stress of the past weeks, I ended up catnapping on the lounger, waking up intermittently when I felt his glare from across the pool.

They were at least keeping it down today, enough so that I could put in my airpods and drown them out with the soundtrack to Mulan. I loved Disney movies, something I knew Mason would mock me for if he knew—not that I gave a shit.

Half asleep and lost in a dream of tender, featherlight touches on my hips and neck, I was startled when I heard, "Hey, Leslie, why don't you join us in the pool?"

I opened one eye, pausing the music. Emory was standing above me, grinning. Mason stood in the pool, while Tiffanie hung off his back and smiled at me. I wanted to say no, to close my eyes and ignore them, but I heard my mom in my head: *Give him a chance. Try to make friends, hon. Do it for me.*

He *was* trying, after all.

So, sighing, I rose off the lounger.

And my bikini slid right off my body, leaving me completely naked in front of a bunch of strangers and my douchebag stepbrother.

Laughter rang out around me. People lifted up their phones, taking photos of me, stark naked and glaring. The only person who didn't laugh was Mason—he looked like he wanted to kill me, instead.

I didn't know why he was so angry, when humiliating me had clearly been his idea.

I shut my eyes, willing the tears away. Yes, I was naked. Yes, it was likely my naked self was going to end up all over the internet and likely destroy my reputation.

I'd had enough.

"You win," I called to him. "I'm the idiot who fell for our 'truce,' but you win. You can have your house back. I'm getting out of here today."

With that, I turned and headed inside, naked, head held high, trying to ignore the splash, high pitched yelp, and pounding footsteps behind me.

Mason caught me around the waist just before I could slip inside the house. I fought him as he dragged me into the kitchen, and continued fighting him when he grabbed his zip-up hoodie from off the back of the chair and forced my arms through it before zipping it up all the way to my neck. It dwarfed me, falling down to my knees. I glared up at him, refusing to be grateful for no longer being naked, refusing to cry.

"What are you talking about, butterfly?"

"You know exactly what I'm talking about. It's not enough to humiliate me—you have to destroy my life, too."

He whipped me around to face him, fisting my hair in his hand—just like he'd done that night in the pool house.

"Don't be so sure of that."

"What, you deny what just happened?"

He didn't respond.

"I think it's interesting that you're trying to deny having any part in it, when it was *your* girlfriend and *your* best friend who did the honors. Or are you saying you didn't know they were going to strip me?"

He stared at me, jaw working, and a secret, pathetic part of me lifted in hope that he'd say no, that he'd apologize, that he'd wreak vengeance on *them* for once instead of *me.*

But he destroyed that when he jerked his head up and down.

"God," I whispered, "Why do you hate me so much? What did I ever do to you?"

"You ruined me," he said. "Irrevocably."

I assumed he meant I'd ruined his life, just by merely existing.

So I also jerked my head. "It's mutual."

"I doubt it."

What the hell did that mean?

"Anyway, you can't go anywhere. Where are you going to go? Last I checked, you didn't have a job; you and your mom live off my dad's money."

I glared at him as I texted Bea.

Can I please come stay with you for the rest of the summer?

I know I'll have to sleep on the couch, but I'm desperate

The stepdemon still causing you trouble?

you know it

yeah, you can come stay here

but what will your mom say?

I'll think of something

"Watch me," I told Mason.

"Oh, butterfly," he murmured, shifting his hand to stroke my cheek and forcing me to shiver from the sensation of his hands once again on my bare skin. "I'm always watching you."

And that's what he did—watched me, as I stormed up the stairs, packed my bags, left a resolute voicemail on my mom's phone—they were in the city for a show and she probably wouldn't get the message until later—loaded up my car, and drove off.

I didn't even see Mason on my way out. If I had my way, I'd never see him again, except for the requisite family holidays like Thanksgiving, Christmas, and, I assumed, his wedding one day where I'd be required to see him marry some poor woman who deserved better than him.

But otherwise, freedom stretched ahead of me. Freedom from his torment.

Turned out I was wrong.

6

MASON

She was gone.

My butterfly had left—flown away, just like I'd told myself I wanted her to.

I was wrong.

I couldn't pinpoint exactly when Leslie had become mine. I'd been resisting how badly I wanted her for so long, I didn't notice when she slipped under my skin and made a home there. Maybe it was the night in the pool, or maybe it was when I'd discovered my skates missing from my closet. I couldn't help how much I respected her for giving as good as she got—even though I had wanted to shake her for it.

Wanted to do a lot more than that. See if she gave as good as she got on her cool sheets in the dark, especially that night when I'd stood in the corner of her room and watched her sleep, vulnerable and unprotected. An unfamiliar urge filled me, to be her protector.

I hadn't wanted to protect anyone, not since my mom faded away in front of me, and nothing I could do could protect her from death, could keep her with me. At that moment, even young, I'd sworn off love, sworn off feeling anything for someone fragile enough to be taken away from me.

But Leslie...she needed someone to look out for her, needed *me.* Maybe it was bullshit for an eighteen-year-old to feel this way, but my instincts told me it was my job to look out for her and provide what no man ever had.

Especially when I heard her murmur the word *Daddy* in her sleep. At first I'd thought it was about her deadbeat father, until a moment later she moaned: My. Fucking. Name.

My cock went hard at the association. My butterfly wanted a daddy? She'd get one.

And then I'd banished the thought, so fucking angry, once again, that she was my stepsister. That as much as I wanted to climb into that bed with her and pull her into my arms, spread those toned thighs wide and massage her pussy until it glistened for me, I *couldn't.* She was my stepsister, and I needed to stay away from her—practically impossible when she had been there all the time, flitting around in beautiful circles, taunting me, just out of reach.

It filled me with so much anger, and I transferred it into my anger at her for stealing my skates. Because the only thing I allowed myself to love was hockey, and now she was intruding on that, too—like a butterfly perching on a pair of skates and completely changing their purpose—a symbol of shelter, not aggression.

So I'd continued to set out to destroy her, even as I got more tangled in her web, hiding my feelings from our parents, from my father's knowing, disapproving eyes. Hating her as much as I—

I banished the four-letter word before it entered my head, instead sighing as I thought back on that day.

I hadn't realized how jealous and bitter Tiffany had

become until Leslie was standing in front of all of us at the pool, naked. I'd been livid. I'd wanted to cover her in a towel, pick her up in my arms, and carry her inside where no one could see her or hurt her, ever again. But if I had, everyone would have seen right through me, and I couldn't give those vultures that kind of ammunition against me. Instead, I stood there and seethed. Leslie must have thought I was angry at her.

And then she yelled at me.

And then she left.

I'd fucked up, badly. Thought I'd wanted one thing, when it turned out I needed something else entirely.

I stood in her empty bedroom, feeling a loss like I hadn't felt since my mom had died.

And swore right then and there that I wouldn't suffer that loss twice. I couldn't keep my mother, but a butterfly could be pinned down, kept—safe and close by.

My father interrupted my thoughts when he stood in the doorway.

"What did you do, Mason?" he asked, his voice quiet.

I shook my head, not bothering to answer.

"I know it was you," he said, voice no longer quiet, but laced with frustration. "I don't know what you did, but I know you did something. Mason, I swear, if you hurt that girl..."

I'd done more than hurt her. I'd tormented her, terrorized her. And, if I were honest, I wasn't done. Leslie wasn't going to like my tactics, even if the end result made it worth it.

"I'll make it right," I swore—to my father, and to me.

"You better." With a last look, he left the room.

I picked up a pillow on the bed, smelling it. It smelled like flowers and sunshine.

I *would* make it right. Leslie was mine, and that meant I'd do everything I could to make her realize it, so we could be together. I was done with protecting my image; it wasn't worth losing her over.

Yes, I'd make it right.

Even if that meant doing wrong.

Speaking of which.

Still holding Leslie's pillow with one hand, I pulled my phone out of my pocket with the other, texting Emory.

You ever pull something like that again, I'll fucking kill you.

He responded immediately.

Got it.

The dots appeared and disappeared as he considered what to say next.

You're serious about her.

As a motherfucking war.

He thumbs-upped what I said.

That done, I messaged Tiffanie on Instagram. I'd already forced everyone at the pool that day to delete all the photos they'd taken of a naked and humiliated Leslie—from their phones and the cloud. I'd also threatened all of them, letting them know that if they'd hidden a photo somewhere, and it got out, they'd have to answer to me. And no one wanted to answer to me. The ways I'd fucked with Leslie wouldn't even compare to the wrath I'd inflict on any and every single one of those assholes.

And Tiffanie? She'd pay for her crimes. I'd known she was up to something, and my mixed feelings about Leslie had stopped me from finding out what. I hadn't noticed her untie Leslie's bikini strings, until it was too late. Tiffanie had gone too fucking far. I was done with her, and she'd learn that—and that fucking with Leslie meant fucking with me.

I DM'd her.

You awake?

Her response was instantaneous.

Yeah, baby.

I pressed the Facetime button, and she picked up immediately.

And she was naked.

"Hey baby," she said in a voice I'd once found sexy.

Now, I was all business. I screenshot her with her hands holding up her bare tits like she could serve them to me through the phone.

"That's all I needed," I told her.

"What?" she asked, confused and pouting.

"I just took a screenshot of you naked, Tiffanie. I'm barely resisting posting it online."

"What the fuck?" the sexy voice disappeared, instead leaving a pissed off girl, close to shrieking.

"If you ever, *ever*, try to hurt Leslie Berger in any way, ever again, I will not hesitate to destroy you with this photo, and anything else I can come up with. Do you hear me?"

She shook her head, hair flying. "Fine, but what the fuck do you see in her, anyway?" She practically spat the words.

I didn't bother to explain. Leslie was funny, feisty, beautiful, with an innocent vulnerability I ached to protect. I was obsessed with more than getting inside what I knew was going to be a tight, hot, wet pussy. I was obsessed with owning every part of her: mind, body, and soul.

"She makes me give a shit," I told Tiffanie honestly. "And if you jeopardize that, there's going to be hell to pay."

Tiffanie sighed. "Well, good luck with that. She hates you."

She wasn't wrong.

"Let me worry about that, and you worry about keeping your head down and that mouth shut, you hear me?"

"You used to like me with my mouth wide open," she said.

I shook my head. "We're over, Tiffanie."

And then, done with that conversation, done with her, I ended the Facetime call. I had more important things to do.

I had a butterfly to catch, after all.

ONE MONTH LATER

7

LESLIE

So far, I'd only been at Tabb University for an hour, and I'd already gotten lost three times. This was slightly embarrassing—I was a city girl and never got lost in New York, no matter where I was, yet the small ivy-covered campus felt like a labyrinth.

Fortunately, everyone had been really nice and helpful as they directed me back to my dorm room for the third time. I dragged the last of my stuff upstairs from the furthest away parking lot since I hadn't been able to get a closer spot. I had a single, which I was excited about. Even though I did want to make friends with the rest of the people in my co-ed dorm, a roommate meant someone who would get annoyed when I woke up early in the morning to stretch and practice...and who might keep me up late at night with their partying.

I was carrying a laundry basket filled with clean clothes when I bumped into a huge, breathing wall and the laundry basket and all my clothes went flying. I also almost went flying, too, except an arm reached out from the wall I'd bumped into and grabbed me.

"Careful there, butterfly," said an amused voice. "You almost lost one of your wings."

I froze, every part of my body screaming no. I looked up—and up, and up. Had he gotten taller?

"Why are you here?" I breathed, unable to gather enough energy to give a real sound to the words. The last time I'd seen him was on the most humiliating day of my life.

"Starting college, same as you. What, am I not allowed to learn?"

"But you're supposed to be at Harvard!"

He shrugged, his hand still on my arm, sending tingles through my body—tingles I did my best to ignore. Like I always had.

"Eh, not anymore. Now, where is all this clothing going to? Seems like you need a hand." He glared at me as I bent over to pick up my clothes and tried to ignore him as I moderated my breathing and considered how to best handle this situation.

"Why are your shorts so short, Leslie? Don't you know we're in public? Anyone can see your ass," he hissed.

"Funny, you didn't seem to care that people could see my ass in the past," I spat at him. "Fuck off, *Mace.*"

Gathering up the last of my no longer clean clothes, I dumped them back in the laundry basket.

He scooped it up before I could stop him.

"Don't call me that, butterfly," he said harshly. "Lead me to your dorm so we can drop this stuff off and you can put on something more appropriate."

"Great, so now you're slut shaming me? On top of everything else?"

He paused for a moment, considering my words. Sighing, he said, "I'm sorry. I'm not trying to slut shame you. If you didn't have me, you could wear whatever you wanted, and anyone who said shit could *eat* shit. But you do have me, and I don't want anyone *looking* at your ass. Or your legs. Not then, not now. These fuckers don't deserve to see them."

He started walking, leaving me standing there, shocked.

Had he just apologized to me?

"Which room, Leslie?" he called back to me, pulling me from my momentary paralysis. I rushed to catch up with him, sure that even though I was leading him to my dorm room, he was leading me straight to hell.

THINGS WERE AWKWARD WHEN WE GOT TO MY DORM ROOM. Being in my dorm room with him reminded me of the night I'd woken up to him in my bedroom this past summer, and that hot, nervous feeling came back. His presence took up so much space, overwhelming, overpowering, and I had to fight my body to keep from swaying toward him. There was barely room to breathe.

He surveyed the room, taking in the photos I'd put up immediately of me and my mom. He ran a finger over one of them, taken at our parents' wedding.

"Some night, huh?" he mused.

"What do you mean?"

He shook his head but changed the subject. "Do you have anything more appropriate to wear?"

"What is it with you and this new obsession with my wardrobe?"

"It's not new," he muttered, then started rifling through my clothes. He held up a dress.

"Why is this so short? Why are all your clothes so tiny? They weren't like this back in Westchester."

How dare he put his hands all over my clothes, or try to control how I dressed? He had no right. *None.*

And I had no reason to get tingly over how irrationally bossy he was being.

Stepbrother, I reminded myself. And also: *I'm a feminist. I don't like this caveman bullshit.*

That done, I focused my attention on the stepbrother in question.

"I'm turning over a new leaf." I'd decided after this summer to embrace my sexuality instead of hiding it. "Mason, stop it!"

I reached over and tried to rip the dress out of his hands. He just lifted it higher up, and since he was at least a foot taller than me at 6'3", it was pretty easy for him to. I jumped, and he caught me, wrestling me backwards until my back was against his chest, his arms wrapped around my waist. I could feel how hard he was. Shock blew through me and my core warmed. I felt myself grow loathesomely wet.

"Well," he murmured, nipping at my ear, "Guess we keep finding ourselves in the same position. What are we going to do about it, butterfly?"

"Nothing!" I tried to shove him away, but all I managed to do was shove my ass against his hardening cock. God, how was he so huge? It was like there was an elephant's trunk back there.

A knock came at the door and then it opened.

"Leslie, do you need help hanging any—oh."

Chris, the slightly creepy RA in my hall—and one of the first people to provide me with directions when I got lost—stood in the doorway, staring at us.

"Who's this?" Chris asked, eyeing us warily.

I tried to pull away from Mason, whose hand just tightened on my waist, almost painfully. He shouldn't be touching me like this, not when someone else could see.

He shouldn't be touching me at all.

"Chris, this is my stepbrother, Mason."

"Stepbrother?" Chris relaxed slightly, then looked confused, his eyes on where Mason still gripped me.

I tugged away and after a moment, he released me, stepping forward to cross his arms and block Chris from entering the room.

"Chris, huh? Why are you here messing with my stepsister?"

Chris puffed up his chest. "I'm not messing with anyone. I'm your *sister's* RA, and I'm offering to help her nail her stuff to the wall."

Mason glared, ice-blue eyes promising pain. I suddenly found myself worrying for Chris' safety. "You won't be nailing anything of hers," he said, his voice filled with warning. "She has me."

With that, he backed Chris out of the room and slammed the door shut before advancing on me.

Oh god, we were alone again. The realization made me breathless. My body was tense, tight, like it was waiting for something.

I focused on what he'd done. "That was rude!"

"He wants to fuck you."

I spluttered, taken aback. He'd lost it. "He does not. And besides, what business is it of yours?"

"Anything that has to do with you is my business. Don't you get that by now?"

I stared at him. I was right; he *had* lost it. Unconcerned with my thoughts regarding his mental state, Mason backed me up further, until I was leaning back against my bed and about to tilt over on it.

And with one solid push to my chest with his big hand, he made sure I did.

I landed on the bed, the breath knocked out of my chest, and Mason climbed up.

Shocked, I just lay there as he prowled over me. "God, you don't, do you? Why do you think I tormented you over the summer?"

"Tortured," I said, voice weak.

"Tortured," he agreed. "Tormented, tortured, did my best to make your life a living hell. It was only fair, you were making my life one, simply by breathing."

I gasped. That *hurt.* I hadn't done anything to him, and he hated me so much. I hated him too, even if part of me wondered what it would be like if our truce had lasted.

"What did I do to make you hate me? Get off me."

He ignored my words, holding his body up in a one-handed push up, so that he hovered over me. Heat spread everywhere from his body to mine, completing the short distance between my skin and his. With his free hand, he started making small, light circles on my inner thighs.

I jerked underneath him, his touch pulsing in my core.

"If I made your life a living hell, why are you here?"

He shook his head, seeming frustrated. "You still don't get it, butterfly. You made my life hell because I couldn't have you. Not when we were both under our parents' roof. But I'm done with that. I'm taking what's mine."

Still shocked and confused—and overcome with more tingles—I started to speak, but he caught my protest with his lips. He bit my bottom lip sharply until I opened my mouth, and then, once he had me where he wanted me, he sank his tongue inside.

Oh god, my *stepbrother* was kissing me.

And it was the best kiss I'd ever had.

He started to fuck me with his kiss. I don't know how else to describe it. He consumed me with his lips, and his tongue made my whole body spark with need. It was so wrong, I knew that, but everything about it felt exactly right. As if every kiss before this one had been off somehow, and this one made all those other ones meaningless.

But that couldn't be right. This was my *stepbrother.* My *bully.*

His hand was still making those devastating little circles on my inner thigh, but it started traveling upward—

"Mason!" My protest was weak. I felt weak and loose, pliant and submissive.

He growled. "That's not what you're going to call me in bed, butterfly. Soon enough, you'll know what I really am to you."

Before I could ask what he meant, he descended back on my mouth and his fingers slid underneath my shorts and panties, until they were touching my bare pussy.

I jerked. No one's hand had ever been there before but my waxer's. It was the best and worst thing I'd ever felt in my life, lighting me on fire.

Mason reared back.

I got it waxed because I liked the feeling of having a naughty little secret, but from the look on his face, he didn't agree.

"Who the hell did you get this done for, Leslie?" he asked, his voice dangerously low. The last time he'd sounded like that, he'd just discovered I'd donated his skates.

"I—I," I stuttered, not sure how to explain.

"I swear to god, butterfly, if you let another man touch *my* pussy, there will be hell to pay. For both you—and him."

His pussy?

His?

More tingles. Fuck my life.

"No one touched me," I squeaked.

"Not even that boyfriend?"

I shook my head. "We broke up."

For good.

He didn't look like he believed me. "Then why did you get your pussy waxed?"

"I like how it feels. I'm a virgin."

Wait a second. This was none of his business, so why was I defending myself like I'd done something wrong? I didn't know why he had this power over me, but I loathed it.

His growl sounded satisfied. "Yeah you are, good girl, but not for long."

He started to kiss me again, and although I wanted to give in, I couldn't. Evil. Stepbrother. Bully. So I swatted at him until he stopped.

"Mason, tell me what's going on. We *hate* each other, and suddenly you want to what, hook up? Is this your newest attempt to mess with my head? Are you recording this? Are people waiting to pop into the bedroom and make fun of me? Is there pig's blood somewhere? None of this makes any sense."

It didn't. Not the way he was talking to me, not the way he was touching me—and not the way I liked it.

His muscles tensed, like he was at war with himself. Then, with a "Fuck!" he rolled off me. My body ached, missing his solid heat, the weight of him on top of me.

"I think you need to leave," I told him, fixing my shorts and ignoring the way that my hand brushed over where his had been, shooting off sparks everywhere.

"I'm not leaving until I fix this," he threatened.

"Leave, or I call your dad and tell him you're trying to

fuck me," I threatened right back, finally finding my strength. I didn't know the details of Mason's relationship with Paul, but the tension between them was obvious. Learning his son was trying to sleep with his stepdaughter certainly wouldn't make things easier between them.

"You wouldn't," he said.

"I would."

We glared at each other, and then with one more snarl, he left, slamming the door behind him. I flopped back down on the bed, confused as hell and turned on as hell.

I didn't understand what had just happened, but I did understand one thing: I wanted it to happen again, even if it made me disgusting.

I was so, so, completely, utterly fucked.

8

MASON

That had gone well.

After slamming out of Leslie's dorm, I considered going to the gym and working out my aggression on some weights, since I couldn't work it out on Leslie's virgin pussy.

Virgin. I groaned and slapped my hand against the wall. She was mine, and would only ever be mine, and all I fucking wanted was to get my mouth on her and find out what *mine* tasted like.

So much had changed since this summer. Since the night I'd met her at the wedding. Leslie had changed everything. Changed *me.* With her sass, her spark, the way she stood up for herself, even though it was clear I terrified her. The sweetness she shared with her mom, sweetness I wanted badly for myself. The submissive way she'd responded to me in the pool that night.

And even though she'd never told me directly, I knew from Paul that her father's betrayal and departure from her life had hurt her, badly. It pissed me off that he could abandon her like that, and it made me understand her better. I'd lost my mom because she died, not because she'd had a second family. Still, I understood what it was like, to be missing that love and stability from your life. We were opposites, mirror images, and would snap together like puzzle pieces—once she let me get close enough.

Yes, she was mine, she just didn't realize it yet.

But she would.

Meanwhile, I had to make sure she was safe, and everyone *else* knew who she belonged to—and to keep their hands off her.

With that in mind, I doubled back, passing Leslie's closed door—where she was no doubt reeling from our interaction. I continued down the hall, ignoring the looks I was getting from the girls standing outside their rooms, barely taking the time to nod at the guys holding out their fists to bump mine.

"Mason, bro! We're going to go all the way to the championships this year with you on the team!" Some freshman said.

"Hell yeah we are!" his friend said, taking the fist bump I'd passed up.

It should've surprised me that people already knew who I was before the year even started, but it didn't. Hockey was huge at Tabb, and my reputation preceded me. In the past, that would have meant everything. Now, I had something that mattered even more than hockey and my ego—and she was only a hallway away from some asshole who wanted to stick his dick in her.

Leslie would never let him, but I didn't trust him. I was her protector now, and like I'd told her RA, no one—no one—would even come close to "nailing" anything.

Driving home that point wouldn't hurt.

"Yeah, man, thanks," I said. "Do you know where the assh—the RA's room is?"

His friend pointed down the hall. "Three doors down on the left, man."

"Thanks." I ducked my chin and continued on down until I reached Chris' room.

I knocked twice—hard and loud.

The door swung open, framing that pitiful asshole as he stared up at me.

"You," he said, disappointed and pissed.

"Me," I confirmed, putting my hand on the doorframe before he could shut the door in my face.

Sighing, he gave in, crossing his arms over his chest to look tough. "What do you want?"

It didn't work.

I shook my head. "Leslie's a sweet girl."

He snorted. "I figured that much out."

I ignored this. "As a sweet girl, she's too nice to enforce appropriate boundaries with men who might want to take... advantage...of her kindness."

His face went red. "I wouldn't ever take advantage," he spluttered.

"No? Well, let's keep it that way. See, Leslie may not be good at enforcing boundaries, but she doesn't need to be."

"Let me guess, because she has you, right?" he scoffed.

"Exactly. Because she has me. You don't want to fuck with me, Kyle."

"Chris."

I ignored that, too. "If I hear from her—or anyone—that you were anything but distantly polite to her, the way an RA should be—you'll have to answer to me. You got me?"

The redness on his face traveled to his neck. "How brotherly of you," he sneered.

This dick.

I didn't bother to correct him again. "You got me?" I repeated.

"I got you. Although from what I observed, it doesn't seem like she really wants you around, does she? Jocks like you always think you'll win. But you may not this time."

I gritted my teeth and counted to ten. Punching this guy before classes even started would get me in a hell of trouble with my coach—and my father, if he found out about it. Chris had heard the threat, and he'd stay away from Leslie... or he'd have me to answer to.

"I'll let you get back to jerking off to sad porn," I told him, wiggling my fingers in a wave. "See you, Kyle."

"Fucker," he muttered, as I stepped away from the door and closed it for him—in *his* shocked face.

That mission complete, I considered my next move with Leslie. She wasn't going to bend easily, or admit that she wanted me, not yet anyway.

"Hi, Mason," a girl giggled, playing with her hair and thrusting her chest out at me.

I wanted to bark at her that I was taken. There hadn't been a hand, mouth, or pussy wrapped around my dick since that night in the pool with Leslie. And there wouldn't be, as angry as my dick was from the lack of action.

That said...

I remembered the way Leslie had reacted to Tiffanie this summer. She wanted me, and if I felt this territorial over her, it stood to reason she felt the same way about me. So I considered my options. If kissing my butterfly hadn't gotten her where I needed her, maybe jealousy would do the trick.

Huh.

Maybe the old Mason—the one who was a dick to my butterfly, and gave attention to other girls—needed to come out for a spin. There was no wake up call like seeing someone else's hands on what was yours. And while Leslie abhorred violence, I didn't. The idea of her scratching some meaningless girl's eyes out for putting her hands on me? That was a cat fight I could get behind.

With that pleasant thought, I whistled, sauntering down the hallway and out of Leslie's dorm, grinning and winking at the girls and nodding at the guys as I went.

Time to use a little bit of that Calloway magic. I'd known I'd need to do some wrong to finally get what was right—Leslie, submissive in my arms.

I couldn't fucking wait.

9

LESLIE

I woke up the next morning for my first day of classes, a complete, exhausted mess. I'd slept terribly the night before, tossing and turning with Mason's words replaying in my head over and over.

I swear to god, butterfly, if you let another man touch my *pussy...*

I was frustrated, uncomfortable, and embarrassingly wet. I took the coldest shower in history, trying to wash his words from my mind and his touch from my body. Afterwards, I stood in front of the mirror of the shared bathroom and tried to do something with my black hair. It was long and straight and hung limply from my scalp.

Ah, well.

A tall, curvy blonde stopped next to me at the sinks and began to apply her makeup. "I'm Lucy."

"Leslie."

She nodded. "Who was that hot guy I saw leaving your room yesterday?"

I blushed. "That's Mason," I mumbled.

"Boyfriend? Ex-boyfriend? Hate-fuck buddy?"

I choked on my mouthwash. "None of the above." Although the last sounded a little too on point.

"Do you want him to be?"

"No!" I must have protested too much because she raised an eyebrow.

"Well, if he's available, let him know I'm interested. He's hot, like, lose your virginity to him and don't care if he ever texts you back, hot."

My eyes narrowed in the mirror. It was bullshit, and I knew it. Hypocritical bullshit, at that. But even though I wanted Mason to leave me the fuck alone, the idea of another woman getting her hands on him...

"He's not available," I said shortly.

God. I was a mess.

She pursed her lips. "Girl, you have to get your shit together," she said, like she'd read my mind and agreed with me. "That is not the man you tug along on a string and expect him to follow. Lock him down, or someone else will."

And with that advice, she finished up applying her lip gloss, blew herself a kiss in the mirror, and left the bathroom.

What did I want? Did I *want* Mason? I obviously didn't want anyone else to have him—a whole can of worms I was afraid to open. My body wanted him, but that was so wrong. He was my stepbrother, and we loathed each other. Which brought up another issue. What if he was just messing with me, and I was falling for his game? I had to protect myself from him, which meant not talking to him. It would be a little hard to avoid him—Tabb wasn't that big of a school—but I was determined not to be alone with him again.

My shitty morning got progressively shittier.

Even though I wanted to avoid Mason, Fate had other plans. She was a petty bitch who obviously wanted me to be confused and miserable and confused some more. Fuck her.

I went to the freshmen cafeteria to grab breakfast before my classes. I played the *Moana* soundtrack to hype myself up for my first day of classes, because nothing said courage like the song "How Far I'll Go."

Lost in the music, I didn't have an eye on where I was going and bumped into a hard body at the entrance to the ivy-covered building.

Stumbling back from the impact, I would've fallen on my ass if the person I bumped into hadn't grabbed my wrist and squeezed. I looked up as I removed my headphones, ready to apologize, and froze.

I really had to stop stumbling into this asshole. Literally.

Mason, dressed in a white vee neck tee that emphasized his pecks and six-pack, stared down at me. He loomed over me, reminding me how tiny I was in comparison to him.

How vulnerable.

"Mason, I—" I began, but the look in his eyes stopped me. Instead of the heat and frustration from yesterday, there was laughing cruelty. It reminded me of the guy I'd met this past summer, the one I'd run away from.

The one I should run from now.

Shoving me away, not gently at all, he laughed, mockery clear and sharp. "Guess even butterflies can be clumsy," he said.

Butterfly had never sounded so ugly coming out of his mouth, and I wanted to slap the mean nickname out of his mouth. Rage—and misplaced hurt—boiled in my chest. I didn't want him calling me *anything.*

His friends, probably all on the hockey team with him,

laughed, too. They continued inside, leaving me behind before I could come up with a retort.

Inside the cafeteria, I grabbed cereal and a banana, wishing I had at least one friend to sit with. I wasn't usually envious of Mason, but I'll admit I felt a small dose of green envy at the sight of him sitting with his friends, surrounded by fawning girls, hips jutted out, giggling as they stood around his table. I tried to rationalize my lack of friends versus his large group of them: Hockey started in October, so he'd likely come early to campus to train, not to mention they all lived together...not to mention that Tabb was a *huge* hockey school, so of course he'd already been crowned king. Unlike me, who knew no one, except for him, Emory, Chris, and Lucy, the girl from this morning.

I didn't envy his popularity, per se, but I deeply and desperately wanted to belong, and right now, I had no one and nothing. That would change once I started my dance classes, it had to—unless Mason somehow wielded the kind of power that would make me a social pariah.

As if he could feel my eyes on his back, he turned to look at me and winked—just as he pulled the girl closest to him into his lap. Her giggle echoed throughout the dining hall and as he dropped a kiss on her neck, I fisted my hands, wanting to disappear.

Which was stupid. Once again, I was feeling territorial about a man I had no claim to—nor did I want one. Why the fuck did I care what he did with girls? He wasn't mine. I didn't like him. If anything, this was better. I didn't *want* his attention, his words whispered in my ear, his hands on my body, his—

Get your shit together, Leslie.

Whatever had happened yesterday had just been another game to him. Of course it had. Nothing had changed; he'd just homed in on a new way to torture me. I refused to give him the satisfaction.

But as she stroked a hand through his hair, I turned around and stuffed my cereal and banana into my bag to eat later. I'd lost my appetite.

10

LESLIE

Even though I'd had plenty of time to make it to my first class, A History of Desire in American Lit, I'd been so flustered by my reaction to Mason in the cafeteria that I got lost three times, despite asking multiple students for directions. Needless to say, I was five minutes late, and unbelievably embarrassed. Punctuality and first impressions were important to me. Just one more thing my stepbrother was fucking up. I doubted I was going to make a good impression on my professor.

So far college was off to a *great* start.

The back door to the classroom was locked, so I had no choice but to walk in through the front—right next to the professor. For a moment, I contemplated ditching class entirely. For a moment, I contemplated packing up and quitting, admitting defeat.

No, fuck that. I'd worked my ass off to get into Tabb, I wasn't about to slink off just because my jackass of a stepbrother was messing with my brain and libido.

Head held high, I opened the door and looked for a seat.

"You're late," the professor said. She was a short, young

woman—honestly, she looked too young to be a professor—who carried herself so well, and had such a commanding presence, I was immediately intimidated and envious. I wanted her to like me. Scratch that: I wanted to *be* her. I wanted the power she had.

I shrugged. "Freshman. Got really lost. Sorry!"

Around me, students laughed. A smile appeared and disappeared on the professor's lips, so fast I almost missed it.

"Don't let it happen again. Go ahead and find a seat."

I looked around the classroom, cursing fate—again. Because there was Mason, sitting in the front of the classroom, next to Emory—someone else I'd never wanted to see again—and the same girl who'd been on his lap an hour ago.

Fuck my fucking life.

He slowly slid his arm over the back of her chair. Intentional? Maybe. Incendiary? Completely. A vision came to me—dragging the girl away from him by her red hair and then punching him in his smirking face.

Controlling my breathing and behavior, I found an open seat in the back of the lecture hall, trying to focus on the professor as she went over the syllabus. It was practically impossible; when I wasn't staring at the back of Mason's head as he laughed at something the beautiful redhead whispered in his ear, I thought about his lips to my ear yesterday as he'd said, "You still don't get it, butterfly. You made my life hell because I couldn't have you. But I'm done with that. I'm taking what's mine." And then he'd consumed me in a kiss.

Was he telling her she was his, right now? Later, would they go back to her dorm room and he'd kiss her like he'd kissed me?

I gripped my pen so hard at the thought, my pen broke, leaking ink all over the paper.

"You okay?" the guy next to me whispered, looking concerned. He was cute—blond curls, blue eyes, a sweet face. He fumbled around in his bag and came up with crumpled paper napkins and a pen.

"Thanks," I whispered back, taking the napkins and pen from him and cleaning the ink off my hands. I wadded up the ink covered paper and napkin and considered chucking them at Mason's head.

"He's a real asshole, isn't he? I hate guys like that. Think they own everything and everyone they come into contact with, just because they were blessed with money and good looks, and they can slap a hockey puck into a net." His cheeks flushed and he glanced at me. "Sorry, that was a bit harsh."

"No, no, it's fine," I said, even though part of me wanted to defend Mason. But he was right. Mason thought everything belonged to him, including me—although I obviously was just a toy to play with and then discard.

Ugh.

Up front, the professor stretched and told us to take a five minute break.

"After, you'll be choosing partners for your first project."

The guy next to me held out his hand.

"I'm Dan," he said.

"Leslie."

I reached out to shake his hand, then pulled mine back. "Sorry, probably shouldn't shake your hand until I know I've gotten all the ink off."

He smiled at me. "You've got some on your face, too."

"Oh my god, where?"

He hesitated. "Can I?"

I nodded. Grabbing another paper towel, he dabbed at my left cheek.

"Got most of it. You may want to go wash it off, though."

"Getting a little friendly with my *stepsister*, aren't you?"

Dan jerked. "Stepsister?" He looked at me, surprised. "I didn't realize you were related. I—"

"Keep your hands to yourself," Mason barked at him, suddenly looming above us. To me he said, "You have ink on your face. Go wash it off."

"Don't you tell me what to do. You don't control me."

"Wanna bet?"

I rose out of the desk and we stared at each other, neither one of us willing to back down.

Which is when the professor joined us.

"Well, this looks intense," she noted. "But this works. Ms. Berger, Mr. Calloway, you've volunteered to work on the first project together—female desire in early American literature." She raised her voice so everyone in class could hear her. "Each of you will find a partner and you'll choose a significant story from the literary canon, and you'll write your own story or script with your partner reinterpreting it. Go ahead, pair up. There may be one threesome."

There were titters throughout the room. I also felt eyes burning into my back, from the girl that Mason had (temporarily, probably) abandoned for his pissing match with Dan.

"Yes, I said threesome. You are all adults now, act like it. Mr. Calloway, if you'll kindly take a seat."

At first, Mason resisted, like he wasn't going to listen to her. But he apparently wasn't the type to rebel against a teacher openly—he'd find sneakier ways to get his revenge. It didn't surprise me; our entire battle this summer had taken place under our parents' noses. Straightening to his full, intimidating height, he then swaggered back to his seat, turning to glance back at me a few times.

Satisfied, the professor looked at me. "Chin up, Ms. Berger," she murmured, then walked back to her spot in the front of the classroom, where she pulled up the rubric on the screen and started talking us through the assignment and expectations.

"I'm so sorry, I didn't realize he was your brother," Dan said, embarrassed.

If he was embarrassed, I was humiliated. I could feel my face turning red. "Stepbrother," I corrected. "And it's fine, he's an asshole."

"Seems like it. He's very, er... protective of you? Or possessive? I don't know, but it was weird," Dan commented.

I blushed harder. This was the last thing I wanted; to be under the microscope like this. Was this why Mason had interjected himself in our conversation? To embarrass me?

Lost for words, I shrugged. "Yeah, I mean..."

"Do you want to try to switch partners? I can tell Professor Evans that you'd rather work with me, and your stepbrother can work with Eric," he offered, motioning to the guy he'd paired up with.

I shook my head, not even wanting to imagine what Mason might do if he found out I was partnering with another guy. He may not want me, but between Dan and my RA, he'd made it clear in less than twenty-four hours that no one else could have me. And besides, there was a part of me —small but insistent—that wanted to work with him. Get to know him in a situation where we weren't adversaries, but collaborators. I hated that I was excited to spend time with him.

And what had the professor meant by chin up? What had she seen in my eyes? In Mason's?

I ruminated over this for the remainder of class. When she dismissed us, Dan asked me if I wanted to get coffee, but I shook my head.

"I should get back to my dorm and get some work done," I told him, forcing a smile. "Maybe another time?"

"Sure," he said easily. "And the offer still stands about partnering up."

"Thanks," I told him.

He walked off. A moment later, Mason appeared at my side. I hated how my body sizzled and then settled, first at the excitement of having him nearby, and the security of knowing he wasn't with the redhead.

"C'mon, let's go get this over with," he snapped.

"Don't talk to me like that," I snapped right back.

"Butterfly, you are testing my patience. Is that what you're trying to do? Do you want my attention? Want me to bend you over this desk and spank your bratty ass in front of everyone who's here?"

"You're disgusting," I said, glaring at him, even though his words sparked something in me.

He got in my space, using a finger to tilt my chin up so he could look directly in my eyes. I shivered from the heat of his body, the touch of his skin to mine.

"Then I suggest you shut your pretty mouth and follow me out this door before it gets you into more trouble," he said.

My sex spasmed at the thought, and his eyes heated.

"You like that, don't you?" he hissed. "I'll keep that in mind."

"I don't," I told him.

"Admit it, butterfly."

"Why don't you go give your attention to one of your groupies?"

He smirked. "Jealous, huh? It's a cute look on you."

Damn it. It was one thing for me to want my stepbrother, it was another for him to know it.

"What-the-fuck-ever."

I stomped out of the classroom, but before I could lose him, he grabbed onto my belt loop and tugged me back.

"Not so fast, butterfly. Don't you want to get started on our project?"

I sighed, even as my own butterflies—the ones in my stomach—danced at the idea of spending time with him. I hated myself for that. He'd been a complete asshole that morning, and my pathetic body and mind still got excited at his nearness. "*Fine.*"

"Let's go to my apartment."

I shook my head. I wasn't a fool. "There's no way I'm letting you get me alone. I don't trust you, and I have no idea what you'll do. We'll go to the library, or I'll march over to Professor Evans' office and tell her I need to work with someone else."

His eyes gleamed. "Library, huh? I'm down for that."

Oh god, why did he look pleased? What had I done?

I shook it off—the library was safe—and started walking to the big, stone and glass building. When he grabbed my hand and linked our fingers together, I inhaled sharply. Warmth shot through me from where our hands were connected. I couldn't remember the last time someone had held my hand, and I doubted it had ever felt like *this*—dangerous and exhilarating and somehow safe, like if I fell, he'd catch me.

Which was bullshit. Mason would happily let me crash on the ground and break all my bones in this metaphor. Damn, he'd probably take pictures of my broken body and heart.

Broken heart?

What the actual hell was going on in my head?

"What are you doing?" I asked him, trying to pull away.

He gripped my hand tighter. "Keeping it so you don't fly away. Don't tell me you don't like holding hands."

"Not with *you.*"

"Liar."

He guided me along the path to the library. Campus was beautiful, surrounded by huge, old oak trees and maples, with sunlight filtering through their leaves. It would've been magical if I hadn't been aware of all the eyes on us. People called hello to Mason, their eyes lingering on our linked hands. Everyone was going to get the wrong idea—especially when they found out we were *stepsiblings.*

With that thought echoing in my head, I used all my strength to pull my hand out of Mason's grip.

"Butterfly, stop," he said sharply.

"People are staring," I hissed. "What are they going to think?"

He looked at me. "Why the fuck do you care what they think? I don't."

I gaped at him. The Mason I knew was obsessed with status, otherwise why did he drive that damn car and surround himself with popular assholes?

"Bullshit," I said.

"Fine," he amended. "I cared what people thought for a long time. But recently I realized that their opinions of me weren't worth it."

Curiosity filled me. "And what changed?"

He looked over at me. We'd reached the library by this point and were standing at the bottom of the steps. I'd been so focused on him, I hadn't even noticed.

"Maintaining my reputation meant I almost lost something incredibly important to me. I hadn't realized it at the time, but after, I decided in order for me to get it back, I had to change my outlook."

"And it's that easy?"

"Butterfly." His voice was low, and warm. "When you crave something this desperately, anything you have to do to get it is easy."

My gut clenched. I had a hunch that he was talking about me, but it was hard to believe that this wasn't just another game. I couldn't trust him, even if his tone made my heart melt a little.

Stupid heart.

"Come on," he said. "Let's go strategize."

11

LESLIE

Mason took me to the fifth floor of the library. The second we stepped out of the elevator, I knew I'd made a mistake. It was empty–just stacks upon stacks of books, with a seductive stillness only broken up by the soft hum of the air conditioner. In between the stacks, a large oak table stood, also empty, like it was waiting for us.

For me.

I shivered. It was a mistake to be alone with my mercurial stepbrother. Whether he wanted me, which was *so* wrong, or hated me, which no longer felt true, this was a bad idea.

"Shouldn't we go where there are more people?" I asked.

He shook his head. "Too loud. I can't concentrate with that much noise." He glanced away, running a hand through his hair. "I have a hard time concentrating as it is. Something my dad always gave me shit about."

It didn't sound like bullshit. It sounded true—and actually, shockingly, vulnerable. Who was the real Mason? The brutally cold douchebag from this summer and this morning? The confident, dominant man with magical hands and lust in his eyes? Or this soft, vulnerable, wounded boy? Was it possible he was all of them?

Softening toward him, I said, "Yeah, I can't study when people are talking. But I usually put my headphones in."

Curiousity filled his face. "What do you listen to?"

Blushing, I looked down. "Disney soundtracks," I murmured.

He grinned, and I prepared for him to mock me, but he just said, "That's cute, butterfly. What's your favorite?"

"*Mulan*. And *Moana*."

He raised an eyebrow. "Not *Frozen?* No 'Let It Go?'"

I laughed despite myself. "I'll admit, I listened to it a lot after you humiliated me this summer."

I'd even choreographed a dance to it with Bea. It hadn't completely canceled out my pain and embarrassment, but it had helped.

"Fucking Tiffanie," he muttered.

I blinked. It wasn't exactly remorse, but I hadn't expected him to be annoyed with his girlfriend. Or ex-girlfriend. "I'm sorry, what?"

"You know, I broke up with that bitch after you left that day," he said.

Ex-girlfriend, then.

"Why?"

"Why?" He took a step toward me. His closeness changed the climate, the setting: the large room became almost claustrophobic, the chill turning to an almost sweltering heat. "Why would I keep eating McDonald's, when there's a five-star, gourmet meal, right within reach?"

My words caught in my throat, and I melted a little more.

God, I really did hate myself. I was a doormat, wasn't I?

"That's a dick thing to say," I pointed out, even if my petty little heart loved it.

He shrugged. "It's true."

Well, I wasn't going to let this conversation go any further. Tiffanie had been a real bitch to me, she didn't deserve a defense. I wasn't sure how I felt about being called a gourmet meal, but I wasn't going to pursue that, either.

Instead, I changed the subject. "We should get to work."

I pulled out my laptop and sat down in the chair furthest away from him. I expected him to sit across from me, and it was discomfiting when he took the chair next to mine and slid it over so our knees were practically touching.

"Do you need to sit this close to me?" I asked.

He raised an eyebrow. "Do you want me to sit on the other side and shout across to you? It's practically in Siberia."

He was wrong, but it wasn't worth the fight.

I opened my laptop. "Okay, what 'canonical work' do we want to write about?"

He shrugged. "That can wait. How are you, Leslie?"

"What, we're exchanging pleasantries now? Let's concentrate on the project. It's the only reason we're spending time together."

He shook his head, his eyes dark. "I want to know how you're doing. First day of class, new school, haven't even gone to ballet yet. You must be stressed. Talk to me."

Why the hell would I talk to you? When you could just use it against me? I wanted to say. But that felt too vulnerable. I wasn't about to show the asshole my hand, even if it had felt good *holding hands* with him.

"How do you think I am?" I asked.

Strong Leslie 1, Doormat Leslie 0.

He shrugged. "I don't know. You've seemed...upset this morning."

"How would you even know? You barely spoke a word to me until class."

"I saw you. You seemed especially upset in the cafeteria. Why?"

I glared at him. He really thought I was that easy. No more Doormat Leslie. "You know why."

"Do I? Oh, was it because Emily was sitting in my lap? I didn't realize you cared."

Damn it. I'd confessed a weakness to him I hadn't even admitted to myself. Well, too late now. But I wasn't going to pretend I hadn't noticed his mood swings with me. He deserved to be confronted, and I deserved answers.

"I. Don't. Care. But yesterday you acted like a caveman in my dorm room and kissed me and touched me, and then this morning you were an asshole and embarrassed me, and now you're acting like I matter to you, that we're friends or something. I can't deal with the emotional whiplash, Mason."

"We're not friends," he said easily. My heart sank at his easy dismissal of me, even though it shouldn't feel anything toward him. "We're more than that," he added, and my heart was buoyed despite myself.

Damn it. Strong Leslie 1, Doormat Leslie 1.

"Right, we're stepsiblings."

"Hmmm."

"Hmm? What's hmm."

"I'm sorry, butterfly," he said. "You're right, my behavior's been erratic. I'll make sure my intentions are clearer in the future. Will that help?"

I blinked.

Had Mason Calloway just apologized? A second time?

"It depends. What are your intentions?"

"I think this is a show, not tell," he said. As he spoke, he placed his big hand on my thigh below my denim skirt. I gulped, suddenly feeling hot all over. He played with the hem, and then his fingers wandered underneath the skirt and...up.

"Mason!" I tried to push his hand away with mine, but he grabbed my wrist with his other hand to stop me.

"Such a bad girl," he tsked. "I can't decide if I should punish you for showing so much skin to so many people, or reward you for making it so easy for me to touch you." He stroked his hand up my thighs, until they rested directly on my underwear, which had grown embarrassingly wet.

"Or are you a good girl? Look how turned on you are by my touch," he crooned, as he started drawing light, teasing circles, around and around.

"Mason. *No*."

"Leslie. *Yes*." He traced a smaller, tighter, more forceful circle around my clit. I gasped and fell back against the chair, the pleasure sucking all the fight out of me.

"Maybe you're both. A bad girl who wore this skirt for my attention, for letting your stepbrother touch you this way. And a good girl for doing what I tell you to do. For spreading your legs and letting me play with what's *mine*."

Mine. The word sang through me, making those butterflies in my stomach riot.

But I couldn't accept his claim, especially when I couldn't trust him. Besides, I belonged to no one but me.

"I'm not yours."

He pinched my clit in reprimand, and I cried out.

"Shhh, you don't want to get caught, do you, butterfly? Or maybe you do. Maybe that's exactly what you want—for someone to see exactly who you belong to." Before I could protest, he slipped his fingers under my panties and thrust one, then two, inside me.

Something no one had ever done before—not even me.

"Fuck, you're tight. No one's touched this virgin pussy before but me. That's what makes you a good girl—*my* good girl. You waited for me," he growled.

As I tried to pull away, to stop him, he pulled me closer, turning his chair and trapping me between his thighs and the table. I had no escape, nowhere to go.

Completely trapped.

And, good fucking god, the realization made me even wetter.

"This cunt is dripping for me," he said, growling again.

He teased my walls with his fingers, stroking in an upward, curved motion that sent pleasure pinging through me like a pin ball machine, lighting up my whole body along the way. He began circling my clit with his thumb at the same time, making my thighs stiffen and my pussy clench around his fingers.

"Ah, fuck yes," he said. "Good girl, do that again."

"Mason," I moaned, despite myself.

"I know, baby, I know. It feels too good doesn't it? Scary good? I can tell because of how tight your pussy is getting around my fingers, and how sloppy wet you are." He hummed as he continued thrusting and circling, thrusting and circling.

Somewhere behind us, I heard the elevator door ding, then footsteps.

I froze, reality intruding. What the hell was I doing?

"We need to stop."

He tsked. "I'm not stopping until you come on my fingers, butterfly. So you better come, if you don't want anyone to see me fingering your filthy, sloppy pussy."

He picked up the pace with his fingers and thumb. Between his touch and the awareness that we could get caught, I was almost a goner. So much pleasure filled me, overwhelmed me, and I couldn't stop it from happening, even if I wanted to. The edge was approaching.

He pressed down on my clit, hard, and I tripped over the edge into free fall.

"That's right. You come for Daddy," he murmured, and I couldn't protest, I was too busy following his orders as my sex spasmed around his fingers and more pleasure than I'd ever felt spilled out of me. At the last moment, he leaned over and captured my cry of pleasure with his mouth and swallowed my desire.

The footsteps faded away, and I practically slithered onto the floor, especially when he withdrew his fingers from my pussy, showed me how wet they were, and then sucked them into his mouth.

"Fuck," he growled. "I can't wait to get my mouth on you."

He placed a soft, wet kiss on my forehead. "Okay, enough fun. Let's work on this project."

As he spoke, outlining our plan, I tried to participate, but I couldn't focus.

"Mason, that can't happen again," I said.

"Sure thing, butterfly," he agreed, easily. Too easily.

And part of me was glad, especially if it meant he could make me feel that way again. As if he could tell what I was thinking, he winked.

"I'll make it good for you, I promise," he said.

I believed him. And I was terrified—not only about how good I'd felt, how I'd *let* him do something so wrong, but that I'd gotten off on it. I'd gotten off on the choice being taken away from me; and from my stepbrother, of all people. I was messed up in the head.

Because I wanted more. More from this man with so many faces and facets. And god help me, I wanted to know all of them, almost more than I wanted his hands on me again.

12

MASON

"Calloway, you're late!" Coach roared as I entered the rink.

He was right. I was late for practice, my fingers still smelled like Leslie's pussy, and I didn't feel one ounce of regret. Not for being late—even though Coach would have my head for it—and not for making my stepsister come, despite the forbidden nature of it, and despite her trying to tell me no.

The only thing I regretted was that my cock was still hard as a rock, even with the cup strangling the hell out of it. It hurt. I welcomed the pain. It would help me focus on my game.

"Where the fuck were you?" Matt, one of my roommates and teammates, asked when I skated up to him.

I shrugged, unable to contain my grin.

He shook his head. "That pussy better be worth it."

Anger shot through me like a puck into the net. I'd known Matt since we were little kids stumbling around on skates together at hockey camp. While he recognized my obsession with Leslie, he'd never understood it—or what she truly meant to me.

Could I blame him? I'd only realized it when she left.

Even so, I had to resist knocking him into the side boards for dismissing Leslie as pussy. Yeah, I fucking wanted her, but I wanted her as more than a cum dumpster. I had plans for my stepsister—the long-term, own-her-forever, lock her down with a ring and plant-fucking-babies in her kind of plans.

Which made it hard not to teach Matt a lesson.

I wasn't the only one thinking of lessons. Coach interrupted me before I could go after my friend.

"Alright, all you assholes. Since Calloway has no respect for things like schedules, instead of today's scrimmage, you're going to do a bag skate."

Everyone stood there, muttering in disbelief. We hadn't been punished yet this preseason. We'd been playing great so far.

Coach raised his voice. "Suicides, all of you."

Fuck.

Glares from the whole team froze me out worse than the ice. This wasn't great. As a new player and freshman, and especially as a second-string center, I hadn't earned my place or respect from the team yet. That would change the first time I got on the ice for an actual game—and proved I deserved to be first—but in the meantime, getting the whole team punished for my lateness was not going to go over well.

Emory eyed me from the net, and shook his head, once.

He knew what I was up to. Maybe didn't condone it, but he'd been my best friend since before we could walk, was ecstatic I was now at Tabb with him, and supported me full out. Even if it meant skating 'til we dropped.

I straightened my shoulders, surreptitiously lifting my hockey glove to my nose. Even though the glove would block the scent, I imagined a faint, sweet whiff of stepsister cunt.

Worth it.

WHEN WE GOT BACK HOME, MY ROOMMATES SLUMPED ON THE couch, utterly exhausted. Emory slid a hand into his pants, texting some girl with the other, while Matt started up a single player shooter game on the X-Box.

I shared a suite with the two of them. We all had our own bedrooms, a massive living room, a private bathroom, and a state-of-the-art kitchen. None of us cooked, but Emory's dad had hired a private chef to make us food when we didn't feel like dealing with the freshman cafeteria. Although I saw my future filled with a lot of cafeteria time so I could keep an eye on Leslie—that was, until she was officially mine, and we could get our own place.

I shook my head, grinning to myself. I was so far gone for that girl. If I thought there was even a chance I was going to be pining from afar, I'd call myself pathetic. Fortunately, there wasn't going to be much pining. Yeah, she was putting up a fight, but she'd already let me fingerfuck her sweet pussy. Just the thought of her wet, tight heat made my cock twitch.

She might push back, but she'd bend in the end.

"How'd it go earlier?" Emory asked. He knew all about my plans for Leslie. He'd tortured her this past summer at my order, even if he'd thought I was fucked in the head. He'd also given me a countless amount of shit over wanting to "fuck your stepsister, you nasty fuck," but once he realized I wasn't budging, he relented.

I ignored him, tossing my keys on the kitchen counter and headed straight to the shower. My cock was pissed—both for strangling it in the cup during practice, and for not letting it out in the library stacks. The sad bastard demanded attention—specifically from Leslie, but since that wasn't an option just yet, my hand would have to do.

Not long though. I was sure of it.

"That good, huh?" Emory laughed.

I flipped him off before slamming the bathroom door closed. In the tiled quiet, I could almost hear Leslie's gasps and cries as she came on my fingers. I was certain it was calling myself "Daddy" that had pushed her over the edge.

I'd never had a Daddy kink—you had to care about someone to want to be her Daddy, and all I'd ever cared about before Leslie was hockey, and getting my dick wet.

My poor cock reminded me it *hadn't* gotten wet. I turned the water on high and undressed.

Leslie was fatherless and tetherless and oh-so-strong, and everything about her triggered a need to control, dominate, protect and nurture—something I'd never wanted with a girl or woman before. With anyone before.

But with her...

...with her...

I took my cock in my hand and started jacking it, imagining hearing her call me Daddy as she kneeled before me, naked, wet, and desperate for me.

I'd jacked off nightly to this very fantasy all summer, although she had no idea. I couldn't let her know the power she had over me. I tried to resist her, to push her away, destroy her—and my feelings in the process. But all that changed that night in the pool—the best and worst night of my life.

I'd fucked plenty by then. But those moments with my cock pressed between Leslie's ass cheeks and my arms wrapped around her tiny waist, feeling her chest heave as she breathed and her body tremble, knowing she was getting wet for me, softening for me—it was the most perfect torture I'd ever experienced.

Something had stopped me from taking it further. Some sense of etiquette or bullshit morality or the good guy syndrome I'd heard of but never been affected by. Even though I felt her go pliant against me, could tell how much she wanted me, I still let her escape. And then I went upstairs and jacked off into the pair of her lacy underwear I'd kept for myself when I'd mailed the rest to her dance studio. That night had changed both our fates. I couldn't resist the pull anymore. I didn't even want to. Instead, I decided to make her mine.

What had been a compulsion to have her near me became something as necessary as breathing. Like I'd said to Leslie in the library, sometimes it took losing someone to realize that their absence was untenable. That you'd give up anything else that mattered to you to have them back.

I pictured Leslie *on her back*, and groaned, working my dick harder as hot water poured over my body.

I'd given up Harvard, something I'd wanted forever, and reached out to Tabb to see if they'd accept a last minute applicant and hockey player. My father had threatened to disown me for it, and I prepared myself for the possibility, researching trade in prices for my beloved car. If I had to ride the fucking bus to make Leslie mine, I'd do it. No task was too big, no life was too small.

Fortunately, I was able to convince Leslie's mother that

this was the best decision for everyone, and she, in turn, convinced my suspicious father to pull strings with the admissions office at Tabb. And based on the way I played in high school, Coach was ecstatic to have me join the team, even as a walk-on.

He probably didn't feel that way today. But I'd get him back on Team Mason.

Leslie had no idea. I swore her mom and my dad to secrecy, telling them it would be a fun surprise, and since Leslie's mom was clueless about the nature of my feelings, and my father was too smart to voice his fears, they went along with it.

Which brought me here, with my hand on my cock. I'd hoped to be balls deep inside her pussy by now, making her clench around me and milk me of all my come, like the good little butterfly she was meant to be. Instead, I was stroking it furiously to thoughts of Leslie's tight, wet pussy clenching around my fingers and the look in those beautiful eyes as she came.

That was all it took. Moaning her name, I shot my release all over the shower tiles. What a waste of come. Once I was actually fucking Leslie, I'd never waste it again.

I had made her miserable this past summer. And she'd given as good as she got, because deep down, she wanted me just as badly as I wanted her. My test with Emily had worked. If she hadn't been jealous, she wouldn't have reacted that way, and she wouldn't have been jealous if she didn't care. She got territorial because on some level, she knew I belonged to her, just like she belonged to me.

She'd convinced herself that she hated me, that I hated her. It was all lies. If she *really* hated me, she wouldn't have let me stick my fingers in her pussy, wouldn't have trusted me enough to come. She wanted my body, at least. The rest would follow. The biggest hurdle would be getting her comfortable with the idea of upsetting our parents and the scandal that would come with being with her stepbrother. I could protect her—I would protect her—but it wouldn't be easy to get her to agree.

However, I'd never *not* gotten something I wanted, and I wasn't starting now. Not with the person who suddenly mattered more than anyone else.

I exited the shower and wrapped a towel around my waist before grabbing my phone.

get home okay?

The bubbles appeared, then:

who is this

you know who it is

mason

I don't know how you got this number

you're my stepsister

you don't think I can get your number easily?

fine

but don't use it again

I glared at my phone. Don't use it again? Fuck that.

nice try, butterfly

what's gotten into you?

other than my fingers

cute

That was better.

I try

The bubbles appeared, then disappeared, then reappeared again.

Mason, what happened today...

Oh, this was the good stuff. I could feel my cock getting hard again.

what about it, butterfly? want a repeat, just say the word

...it can't ever happen again

What the fuck was she talking about, it couldn't happen again? I knew she was resistant to me, I knew she had good reason to be, but I wasn't going to accept this.

why

you know why

careful, butterfly

goodbye, Mason

No. Fuck that. I barely resisted throwing my phone against the wall. She was skittish, and it was understandable. I'd hurt her, she thought the naked photos were my idea, and she was worried about what people would think. I'd get her past that, I just needed to be creative.

I wandered out into the living room.

"Matt, do you still have access to that new drug?"

Matt always had access to the good shit, even the newest stuff. Even the stuff that had purportedly been developed by the mafia.

Emory shook his head. "This isn't the way, Mace."

"Don't fucking talk to me about the 'way' until you find a woman you want more from than sex."

Emory shook his head. "Whatever man, you do you."

Actually, what I was going to be doing was Leslie, but I didn't bother to correct him. I had more important things on my mind.

"Do you?" I prodded Matt.

He twisted his head around. "Which one, bro? Vixen or Vice?"

"Both."

13

LESLIE

"Tondue, tondue, plié, plié, ran de jambe, grand plié," Madame Poirot, the ballet instructor, directed the class. She was, in fact, much too young to be addressed as "Madame"; a young Black woman in her twenties with braids wrapped into a bun, and a tight purple leotard gracing her athletic body. She'd seemed kind at first, until we jumped into exercises, and then the strict ballet teacher came out.

We'd been at it for two hours. I was dripping with sweat, my thighs and calves were burning, and I hadn't felt this peaceful since I'd first bumped into Mason yesterday. Ballet kicked my ass, and I loved every second of it.

What I didn't love was the way Emily kept turning around and glaring at me while talking to her friends. Yes, just to make my day shittier, the redhead who'd sat on Mason's lap during breakfast was not only in my dance program, but in my class. Which meant I was going to have to see her *all the time.* I really needed to have a talk with Fate.

I tried to ignore her, throwing myself completely into the exercises. My body was going to hate me in the morning because in some ways I was completely overdoing it, especially for just a class most of the dancers were marking their way through. But the more my muscles burned, the more I strained for perfection, the less my brain tortured me with images of the two of them together. It certainly couldn't doubly torture me with its taunts asking why I cared who Mason was with in the first place.

Or triply torture me by reminding me how good it had felt when he had played with me in the library. My whole body went clammy at the memory, and this time the sweat pouring off me had nothing to do with ballet.

"Alright, class, take a break," Madame Poirot called. "You deserve it."

Leaning back against the barre, I opened my water bottle and chugged.

"Oh, it's the pathetic stepsister, isn't it?" Emily sneered in front of me, flanked on two sides by her perfectly coiffed friends.

Shocked that she'd gone from passive aggressive glares to outright confrontation, I choked on my water, gagging and spitting it all over my leotard—and her ballet shoes. I couldn't pretend I didn't take some satisfaction in that.

"What the hell?!" she shrieked. "Oh, you little bitch."

I straightened my back. She thought she was the shit because she had Mason's attention. But I'd dealt with his girls before, and *they* were the pathetic little bitches, not me. I remembered Tiffanie, so absurdly jealous she'd taken naked photos of me. I'd always thought that Mason was the one who had told her to take them, but now I wondered: if that were the case, why had they never been posted online? Was it possible she acted without his knowledge?

Emily snapped her fingers in my face, bringing me back to the present.

Right, this bitch.

"That was an accident," I said calmly. "I'm sorry for spitting on your shoes, but I'm not sorry for anything else. I don't know why you have a problem with me, but get out of my face—now."

She sneered at me, looking me up and down. "I'll tell you the problem I have with you. You're disgusting, crushing on your own *brother*, you skank. You're conceited and delusional if you think he actually wants you."

Well, I had proof that he wanted me, didn't I? Unless I'd been right and I was just a game to him.

As if she'd heard my thoughts, she smiled. "Any attention you think you've gotten from him is just him fucking with your head. How could he want his silly little, loser stepsister? What do you think you have to offer him, except boredom and ridicule?"

I tried to calm my breathing, willing my face not to turn red. No luck; I could feel my cheeks heat with embarrassment, especially because I could feel everyone's eyes on me.

"Tell you what," I said to Emily, "You may think I'm delusional, but you're making up some false story to deal with your own insecurities—that you can't hold onto Mason, and that he's using you. Unlike you, I want nothing to do with him. All of the attention I get from him is his choice. Can you say the same for yourself? Or are you another girl throwing yourself at him? Let me let you in on a little secret: he's not worth it. Promise."

With that, I turned back toward the barre and ignored her for the rest of class. I wasn't going to let her tear me down or chase me away. I'd let someone do that before—Mason and his friends, when they tortured me enough to run off to Bea's for the remainder of the summer. I wasn't letting anyone do that again. It didn't matter that Emily thought I was pathetic, *I* knew I wasn't.

Then why did you let your stepbrother stick his hand up your skirt and get you off? my inner voice asked, half-taunting, half-curious.

That question plagued me for the rest of class, as I ignored the glares and whispers directed my way. It trailed me as I walked back to the dorm, torturing myself over my actions earlier that day. Forget what everyone here would think, what would my mom say if she found out I'd hooked up with my stepbrother? Her husband's son? Shame snuck its way into my dorm room with me, where I collapsed onto my bed and muffled my frustrated scream.

My phone buzzed, interrupting my flip out.

get home okay?

The text was from a number I didn't recognize.

who is this

you know who it is

Goddamn it. How had he gotten my number? He was the absolute last person I wanted to talk to right now, even though those butterflies danced in excited circles in my stomach. They must have been high.

mason

I don't know how you got this number

Another text came through.

you're my stepsister

you don't think I can get your number easily?

Fair point.

fine

but don't use it again

I tossed my phone down the bed, but it buzzed again.

Don't look, I told myself.

But I couldn't stop myself from picking it up again and peeking at it through my fingers like it was a horror movie.

nice try, butterfly

what's gotten into you?

other than my fingers

Heat stirred in my stomach and between my legs. His crude words brought back the memory of his hands on me, and how good they had felt. But I couldn't let him know I felt that way.

cute

I try

I started to smile at that, but froze when I remembered the sneer on Emily's face, and the judgment I could feel from everyone listening to our confrontation. I had to stay away from Mason. Even if this wasn't just a new way to fuck with my head. Even if I was right that Tiffanie had acted of her own volition this summer. Even if Emily was full of shit.

Mason had once told me I'd ruined his life. Well, if I kept letting him play his games, he would ruin mine. I was sure of it.

Mason, what happened today...

what about it, butterfly? want a repeat, just say the word

I swallowed, typing words I didn't totally believe. But I had to.

...it can't ever happen again.

There was a pause in the conversation, then he responded.

why

you know why

careful, butterfly

goodbye, Mason

This time, I turned off my phone and slid it inside the drawer in the nightstand next to my small bed. I buried my head in the covers. I should've felt relief, right? Instead, I felt unspeakably, inexplicably sad.

Someone knocked—tentatively—on my door. The butterflies started up again...could he have gotten here so soon?

Yeah, you really seem like someone ready to say goodbye, that inner voice scoffed. I shushed it, opening the door, preparing to tell him to leave.

I was annoyingly disappointed to see it wasn't Mason, but instead Chris. I leaned away immediately, trying not to completely recoil at his smell: slight BO and a pretty strong stench of alcohol. I knew drinking was a big part of college, but it was only 4 p.m. And he was alone.

"Leslie!" He slightly slurred the "s" in my name. "What's happening?"

"Um, nothing, just resting," I said.

"Cool, can I come in? Or is your douchey brother here?"

"Stepbrother," I corrected immediately. "But no, he's not."

"Great." He stumbled past me, sitting—or rather, falling—onto my bed. I wrinkled my nose. I didn't want his stench all over my bedding.

"Chris, why are you here?"

"Figured I'd lend you a hand if you needed anything else set up or nailed in your room." He snorted at his own gross joke.

"No, I'm good."

"Aw, don't be like that."

I swallowed. "Chris, are you drunk?"

He sat up. "No, of course not." His hiccup contradicted this.

"Chris, please leave my room. I don't feel comfortable with you here."

"And what are you going to do about it? Sic your jock stepbrother on me?"

I had no idea if it would work. Mason had taken issue with Chris earlier—in fact, his interaction with Dan from lit class proved he didn't like it when other guys talked to me *at all.* But I had no idea if that extended to confronting or threatening my creepy, drunk RA. I also didn't know if I had any other way to warn Chris away from me.

It fucking pissed me off, how little power I had.

"He's super protective," I said quietly. "He won't like you bothering me."

Chris spat on my floor. "Fine, you're clearly in a mood. I'll come back at a better time, cutie."

I stood by the door, watching warily as he stood up and stomp-stumbled his way out of my room. As soon as he was gone, I slammed the door shut, locked it, and slid down onto the floor, burying my head in my hands. Should I report him? Or would that cause more trouble for me? College was supposed to be fun, wasn't it? So far, it was more stressful than this summer had been.

On impulse, I grabbed my phone out of the drawer, powered it back on, and told Siri to Facetime my mom.

A moment later, her face appeared on screen. She was in the kitchen, her face and hands covered in flour. She was grinning wide as she brushed her blonde bangs out of her face.

"Honey! How was your first day?"

"Hi Mom," I said, settling back against the wall and forcing a smile on my face. "It was good."

"Yeah? Have you made any friends? How are your classes? Have you seen Mason?"

I nodded. "There's a girl in my dorm, Lucy. She's nice." Mom didn't need to know we'd barely spoken. "Ballet was good—I love the instructor. And I have an American lit class I like so far."

It didn't *really* count as lying if I didn't say that Mason was in my class, right? It was only omitting a fact.

"Oh, good. I'm glad you've made a friend. I know it's

hard, being in a completely new setting—but you'll find your group soon enough. And that stepbrother of yours should help—he promised us he'd watch out for you."

"Yes, he did," said Paul, and then the phone camera turned to show my stepfather in a suit and glasses. He, too, had flour on his clothes, sticking to his lapel and marring his otherwise pristine button down. "Has he been treating you well?"

I hesitated. I could tell Paul right now what his son had done. He didn't know about Mason's antics this summer, and certainly didn't know about what had happened in the past forty-eight hours.

I hadn't told them this summer because I was worried friction between us would weigh on my mother's new marriage, and I desperately wanted her to be happy. After the way we'd learned that we were my father's second family, and she was, essentially, his side piece, she deserved some joy in life.

God, my father, that fuckface. Proof that there were very few good men out there.

"Leslie?" Paul prompted, a frown appearing on his face and between his eyebrows.

I could tell. I should tell him. He'd intervene, punish his son, maybe even threaten to stop paying for school if he continued to be a dick.

I could. But I remembered the embarrassed look on Mason's face when he told me he had a hard time concentrating, and that Paul "gave him shit about it." And even though Mason was unequivocally an asshole, I couldn't put him in a position where his father hurt him again...especially after he'd confessed something so vulnerable and private.

"He's been very helpful. And kind," I added, because if I was going to lie, I was going to throw my whole self into it.

Paul snorted. "Mason, kind. That's a first."

"Paulie!" my mom interjected off-screen. "Don't be cruel. He's changing."

Paul shook his head. "I'll believe that when I see it. Here, I'll pass you back to your mother."

The phone shook as it turned, and I heard whispering and my mother's laugh. This time, my smile wasn't forced.

"You sound happy," I told her when she was back on camera.

"I am, honey. All I want is for you to be happy too, okay?"

I nodded. I wasn't sure if happiness was in the cards for me anytime soon. "Okay."

After we said our love you's and hung up, I stared at my phone, clicking back to the text chain with Mason.

He'd read the last text, but hadn't responded, and if I were honest with myself, it made me sad.

But it was for the best.

Even if it hurt.

14

LESLIE

It was Wednesday, AKA lit class, AKA I'd have to see Mason again. As I got ready in the bathroom, Lucy scampered in.

"Shit, shit, shit," she muttered, headed straight to the toilet stalls.

I grinned to myself. A minute later, the toilet flushed and she headed over to the sinks next to me to wash her hands. She groaned when she looked at her face in the mirror.

"I'm so fucked."

"Late to class?"

"Worse. I'm hungover and I have a meeting I'm already fifteen minutes late to. And the C— he'll be *pissed*. And my head hurts too much for one of his lectures."

The way she'd cut herself spiked my curiosity. "Who's 'he?'"

She threw her hair in a top bun and brushed her teeth furiously, speaking around the toothbrush. "My neverending nightmare. My warden. My jailer. It doesn't matter, he's going to make my life a living hell for this."

"You're being really vague. And kind of sketchy," I observed, amused.

She snorted. "Like you aren't sketchy about your stepbrother. Tell you what, I tell you about my personal hell, and you tell me about yours. Deal?"

I waffled. I'd already called her my friend when I was talking to my mom. It would be really nice if I could call her my friend for real. But could I trust her? Wouldn't she judge me?

"Believe me, anything you've done doesn't come close to what I've done—or what I want to do," she muttered. "Judgment-free zone here."

I smiled. "I'll think about it. But you should probably get going."

"Fuck!" With that Lucy spat out the toothpaste, wiped her face down with a towel, and tossed her shower caddy at me. "Can you hang onto this for me? I'll come get it later, I have to go or I'm going to be sent to a damn convent. And I'm *Jewish*. That's how bad this is gonna be."

I laughed. "So am I. And sure. Room 312."

She put her finger to her forehead as she backed out of the bathroom. "312. Got it, see you later, fellow Red Sea pedestrian, and thank you!"

Once she was gone, I sighed, feeling better than I had in a while. Maybe I *could* trust her.

But first I had to deal with seeing my *own* nightmare, as Lucy had so aptly put it.

When I got to class, Mason was already there. I made sure to take a seat as far away from him as possible—and the asshole stood up, grabbed his stuff, and crossed the room to take the seat next to mine, a coffee in his hand. I gaped at him, aware the whole room was watching, including the row of girls who clearly wanted him to sit by them, based on the way they glared at me.

At least Emily was out today. Thank goodness for small favors.

"What are you doing?" I asked him.

He didn't answer, handing me the coffee.

I gaped at the coffee, too.

"Is it poisoned?"

He laughed. "No. Not even with almond milk. I had to go to three coffee shops to get you a lavender latte with oat milk."

"You know what my coffee order is?"

"Butterfly, I know everything about you."

With that jaw-dropper, he sprawled out in the seat next to mine, his leg butting up against my own.

He knew my coffee order? The *butterflies* in my stomach started to dance excitedly. He went to *three* (three!) coffee shops to get me exactly what I wanted? And of course, the latte was delicious. It tasted better than any I'd ever had, and try as I might, I couldn't pretend it didn't send warmth through me—and it wasn't just the liquid, either. It felt like care.

Had a man ever shown care like this to me before?

This couldn't be real.

What was Mason playing at?

"Short shorts, again?" he said darkly, but at least this time he didn't lecture me.

No, what he did was worse. He started playing with the hem on my shorts, his touch transporting me back to the way his fingers had felt inside me. I grew embarrassingly wet.

"Stop it," I hissed.

"Hey." He shrugged. "You wore them. I can't help that your legs are too sexy to keep my hands to myself. Can you blame a guy?"

Actually I could, and I was about to say something, when Professor Evans cleared her throat.

I tried to pay attention to what she was saying about the reading, but I kept getting distracted by Mason's fingers whispering against my outer thigh. If that weren't enough, he'd leaned his whole body into mine, so his arm brushed up against the side of my breast. The room was hot but my nipples still hardened, and I knew Mason saw because his nostrils flared and his breathing quickened.

We might as well have been alone in that room. Everyone else ceased to exist. All I could pay attention to was the heat pouring off of Mason's body, the way his barely-there touch made me crave more. His lips quirked, like he knew what I was thinking, and I wanted to either punch or lick them, I wasn't sure which.

"Pay attention, butterfly," he murmured into my ear.

And then he bit it.

Heat flooded my core, making me wet from the shock of his bite. I trembled all over.

"Stop it," I hissed.

In retaliation, his hand traveled from its moderately safe spot where it was tangled in my shorts hem, up over the top of my thigh to my inner thigh, and then..

And then...

And then he eased his fingers into my shorts. No one was looking, thank god, but as his fingers trailed their way up to my pussy, running over the seam of my panties, I had to bite my lip to contain the gasp that threatened to let loose. Since when was I an exhibitionist?

His fingers paused, a threat all of their own.

And even though I knew I had to shove his hand away, or scream or something—he was my stepbrother, for god's sake, and I hated him, and we were in public! More public than the library!—I couldn't bring myself to, just held my breath as he once again eased his fingers where they didn't belong—underneath my panties so that they brushed my bare sex...just like Monday.

"I've changed my mind about your naked pussy," he whispered, moving his pen around with his other hand like he was actually taking notes. "Now that I know no one's been there, I like how sexy it feels to have nothing between my fingers and your skin." His fingers trailed between my lips. I knew he could feel how wet I was.

He growled again, and I must've had some Pavlovian response now to that growl because I grew even wetter.

"All this for me, butterfly? You shouldn't have."

I shuddered in my seat as his fingers began to circle my clit, barely there brushes at first that began to heighten in intensity. I felt myself clenching and releasing, clenching and releasing, as my core tightened almost painfully, my nipples beaded, and I began to climb that mountain toward orgasm.

"Are you paying attention to the professor, butterfly? You don't want to make a bad impression the first week."

"Ms. Berger?" The professor called my name.

"Uh, yes?"

"What are your thoughts on the reading?"

The reading? Oh, right. I could barely remember what I'd read in preparation for class, so distracted by Mason, whose fingers had picked up in speed and intensity. And now everyone was watching. Could they tell what was happening?

God, I was going to come. In *class*. They were going to expel me, and Mason was just going to laugh.

"*The Awakening*, butterfly," he prompted under his breath.

"It was interesting," I squeaked, trying to shove his hand away. Instead, he just gripped my pussy tight in punishment, like he was claiming ownership.

"Mmhmm," the professor said. "Interesting, how?"

I turned beet red, fumbling for something, *anything,* to say. "Well, the fact that so many women who embraced their sexuality and finding something for themselves, end up committing suicide in literature. I get that it's supposed to be commentary, but what about them living happily ever after? Why do women always get punished for having good sex?"

People around me tittered. *Oh god,* I'd just humiliated myself.

"Hmm," said the professor. "Interesting, indeed."

She turned away to call on another student, and I released a relieved breath—or started to—but Mason had caught my clit between his fingers.

"Punished for having good sex," he murmured, turning to look at me. As I stared into his deep blue eyes, entranced by the need I saw in them, he pinched. *Hard.* All the blood rushed to that tiny but powerful spot, and something about the combination of pain and pleasure, and the intensity in his eyes, made me almost tip over the edge—

—just as everyone started gathering up their things.

Class had ended and I hadn't even realized.

He released my clit and withdrew his hand, wiping my wetness on my bare thigh. I wanted to scream out of need and frustration. To beg.

But I wouldn't beg. Not him. Not ever.

"I'd lick my fingers, but that might be a little obvious," he told me, winking. "No coming."

He gathered his things, dropping them in his backpack and slinging it over his shoulder. I stared after him in a state of confusion and desire.

I needed to come so badly, but for some reason, I listened to him. He'd broken something in me, and was slowly rebuilding it to his specifications.

I didn't know how to stop him.

I wasn't even sure I wanted to.

15

MASON

I got back to the suite and headed straight for the shower. It only took three pumps of my hand until I was coming all over the tiles. At this rate, we were going to have to call a plumber soon; jizz was terrible for pipes.

I leaned against the wall, heart racing, letting the water wash it away. I hated wasting it, yet here we were again. All of my come should go in and on Leslie, and I promised myself that next time, it would be inside her—cunt, mouth, or ass, or maybe all three, I wasn't choosy.

Just the thought of filling her three holes made me hard all over again, and

I had to beat off until my cock felt rubbed raw. Still, I didn't feel satisfied, but it would have to be enough for now.

My plan was working. She was so turned on, she hadn't stopped me, which was the important thing. I had a hunch that she wouldn't go against my order, at least as long as she could. But I didn't believe in hunches. Fortunately, I'd prepared for this. Before move-in day, I'd bribed an assistant in the housing department to give me Leslie's dorm room information so I could hide cameras in her room. I'd also put a powdered aphrodisiac called Vixen in her latte. Even though Emory had disapproved, Matt had gotten me in touch with his contact at Reina U—Jack Feldman, left wing for the Reina University Kings. The Kings were our team's main rival, but if Jack knew a dealer with easy access to Vixen and Vice, engaging with him was a necessary evil.

The gossip was that Jack had ties to the mafia, and that one of his older brothers was a Navy SEAL-turned-hitman, and the other was a billionaire. Rumors aside, Jack was a sociopath. He made *my* actions look downright saintly. I didn't give a shit who he was related to. He'd gotten me the name of a dealer who had the drugs I needed, and for that, I was grateful.

Not that I'd take it easy on him when we played his team.

One dose of Vixen had cost me a fortune, but it was worth it. It took about 3 to 4 hours to go into effect. But by tonight, my butterfly would be desperate. Probably so desperate that she wouldn't be able to follow my order not to come for long.

I couldn't fucking wait.

Emory could go suck a dick. I knew he was looking out for me, and wanted me to try to take a slower, more rational approach. And I'd been willing to, until she'd told me goodbye. That wouldn't do. I knew I was being an asshole about this, but I didn't care. The best thing for Leslie was to be with me, to let me take care of her. I'd heard about the confrontation with Emily in her dance class on Monday, and the fact that Leslie hadn't come to me to help—or at least called me out on Emily's accusations—was unacceptable. We belonged together, and getting her to lower her inhibitions and be with me, full out, no restrictions, no doubts, was the only way to get us there. The first step, but a necessary one.

Who cared if it was illegal?

Who gave a shit if it was fucking unethical?

What did it matter if I was going to hell for it?

I'd promised myself I'd do anything to make Leslie mine—and this was part of the anything.

My phone buzzed, distracting me.

Did it work?

It was from an unfamiliar number with a New York City area code.

who the fuck is this

Jack Feldman. Did the Vixen work?

Speak of the fucking devil. He even used punctuation like a sociopath. Who the hell used periods and capitalization in text messages?

why don't you know that yourself

Haven't tested it on anyone. Haven't found the need to, yet. Your girlfriend is my guinea pig.

Alarm briefly swept through me. Vixen was an aphrodisiac, but it shouldn't physically harm Leslie. If it seriously hurt her...

I swear to god Feldman this shit better not have long term negative effects or I'm going to come to Reina's campus and shove my stick up your ass

turn you into a human shish kabob

That's a nice visual.

Don't worry, it shouldn't hurt her.

The only person who's going to be hurting your girlfriend is you.

I swallowed, unsure how to respond. Although I felt some relief at the confirmation that Vixen wasn't going to have long term ill-effects on Leslie, Jack just putting it out there caused me a moment of self-doubt. Drugging her to get what I wanted was fucked. I knew it, Emory knew it, and Jack *clearly* knew it.

And then another text came through:

That's not a bad thing, if it gets you both what you need. But you need to be honest with yourself about what you're doing.

I relaxed. He was right. So I asked,

why do you keep calling her my girlfriend

If you wanted to score some Vixen and Vice so you could take advantage of some unsuspecting girl at Tabb who doesn't matter to you so you can get laid, you're a pathetic incel jackass who doesn't deserve to fucking breathe. But if she matters to you, and deep down, you know this is something she needs, but this is the only way you can get her there…then I'll let you live.

I stared down at my phone, shaking my head.

Enjoy the Vice, too. You can tell me all about it when we beat you next month.

There was no way in hell I'd let his team beat us.

whatever man

i'm not telling you shit about my dick

and you're not gonna beat us

Okay.

See? Complete sociopath. And yeah, it takes one to know one.

Still, he was right.

So I went to my bedroom, popped a Vice (another black market drug that was basically Viagra on steroids; no refractory period, no side effects), opened my laptop, navigated over the application that accessed the cameras in Leslie's room, wrapped my fist around my cock, and settled in to watch the show.

Leslie's dorm room was empty. Where was she?

As I waited, I scrolled back to yesterday's footage. What I saw had my jaw stiffening and my cock going soft. I watched in rage as that asshole RA forced his way into her room, collapsed on her bed without her fucking permission, and said something that clearly made her upset. I cursed myself for not installing mics, so I could hear what he said. No matter, whatever it was had made her uncomfortable, and no one made my butterfly uncomfortable but me. Leslie's RA was about to learn a very important lesson: You don't mess with what's mine without consequence.

As I ran through ideas of how to handle him, the door to Leslie's room opened and she appeared in the camera. As she frantically pulled off her clothes, I settled in to watch the show.

The RA could wait. Seeing my stepsister lose her inhibitions to the drug in her system? And then giving her exactly what she needed, exactly how she needed it? That took priority.

But I'd deal with him later. He wouldn't fuck with her again, not when I was done with him.

16

LESLIE

I desperately needed to come. But when I got back to my dorm room, stripped down to my underwear and lay on my bed, something stopped me from reaching under my panties and touching my clit.

I'd always been too embarrassed to touch my clit without underwear on, even by myself when I knew no one would see me, and I couldn't seem to rid myself of that silly embarrassment now. I also couldn't bring myself to get myself off. It was like Mason's order had latched onto my brain and I had no choice but to listen to him.

My only class today had been our lit class. Afterwards, I'd gone to the dance studio to try and work out some of my frustration. After an hour of pushing my body to extremes, I was no less frustrated. My body burned, my panties were soaked, and I needed to come so bad I wanted to scream. My clit physically hurt.

Who the hell cared about Mason's demand? I needed to get myself off.

The second my fingers touched my clit, I convulsed in an orgasm. Everything tightened and released so quickly I was worried. But when I was done, the relief wasn't there. In fact, it only got worse.

I started rubbing my pussy—direct contact this time—needing to get off again and for the desperate desire to go away. There was something freeing about my desperation; I needed another orgasm so badly, my shame about taking pleasure in my own body no longer mattered. If I'd been fully coherent, I would've marveled over it, maybe celebrated it. But the desire was too overwhelming. And every time I got myself off, I just needed more, and more.

After what felt like hours, I ended up curled into a ball on the bed in tears, my hand between my legs, completely raw. My pussy walls clenched around nothing. I needed more than an orgasm, I needed human contact. *Connection.* And as scared as I was, there was only one person I wanted it from.

Someone knocked on my door.

Oh god, what if it was Chris?

The knock came again. "Butterfly," Mason called.

Relief filled me. I'd felt so empty. But he. Was. Here. I'd needed him, and he'd come. I went to unlock the door, uncaring about my nudity. There he stood in jeans and a sweaty t-shirt. He smelled musky and filthy and I wanted him all over me.

He growled but gently guided me back into my room and away from prying eyes, shutting the door.

"How are you doing, butterfly?" he asked, his voice tender.

"I need you," I cried.

"Yeah?" He stepped into the room, closing and locking the door behind him. An alarm bell sounded in my brain, but it felt dreamlike and far away, especially once he backed me up against the bed like he had that first day.

Except this time I wasn't confused, or ashamed.

This time, I didn't doubt myself.

This time, I could admit how badly I wanted him.

"You need Daddy, butterfly? Need him to make you feel all better?"

Suspicion made its way through my sex-soaked, horny-blurry brain.

"How did you know that?"

"Because I know everything that goes on with *my* pussy," he said. "I especially know when she needs her Daddy."

Each time he called himself Daddy, my thighs clenched. He'd called himself Daddy before, and my body loved it as much now as it had then. I didn't know *why* I liked it, and I was too horny, too desperate, to care.

His eyes swept my bare torso and lace encased breasts and sex. I was wearing a sheer bralette, and my nipples showed through it. His eyes went dark with lust. He'd seen me naked before, but this was different—we weren't surrounded by his asshole friends and I wasn't angry or humiliated.

"You're so fucking hot," he said fiercely. "More perfect than I could have even imagined."

Then, before I could protest—not that I would at this point—he lifted me up onto bed, placing me carefully on the center before climbing up next to me.

"I want to defile your sweet body," he told me, "but you're a virgin so I'm going to take it easy on you."

"Please," I begged him, uncaring anymore what our history was, or how mean he'd been to me, or how wrong this was. "Just make the pain go away."

He shushed me. "Of course, butterfly. Daddy will make it all better."

And then he parted my legs, pulled my panties off my

writhing body, placed my feet on his shoulders, and leaned down to stare at my pussy.

"God." He breathed me in. If I'd been in any other state of mind, I'd be self-conscious. Instead, I cried out. "I knew you'd be beautiful, but I had no idea you'd be this beautiful, Leslie."

He placed a gentle kiss above my clit. I squirmed, and he smacked my thigh in reprimand.

"Still," he commanded, holding my hips tight with his big hands so I couldn't move around. It made it all the more intense when he licked from the bottom of my slit to the top of my clit.

And then he licked again.

And again.

Heat flooded me, and I started saying nonsensical things, silly sounds broken up by his name, especially when he stuck his tongue in my pussy and began to truly eat me out.

"Mason!" I cried.

"You don't call me Mason," he growled, making that Pavlovian response go off again. "You call me Daddy when we're in bed, butterfly."

"Daddy," I cried, not caring that I was giving in so easily. I needed him too badly.

In reward, he licked, sucked, and bit until I screamed as I came again, and again, and again.

It was better, but it still wasn't what I needed.

"Please, please, please," I begged him.

"What do you call me?" His mouth was covered in my juices.

"Please, Daddy, I need..."

"Shh, butterfly. I know exactly what you need. You need Daddy's big cock, don't you? Need it to stuff you full and fill you up with his come? Don't worry, it'll happen, but first you have to give Daddy a little something."

Picking me back up, he deposited me on the floor. I stumbled, and he caught me.

"Time to get out of this bra," he mused, peeling it off me and dropping it on the floor. And his face changed to something so terrifyingly animalistic, I should've run. Instead, I whimpered.

"Yes," he snarled. "There are those perfect little tits. Look at how hard and red your nipples are. They want me just as badly as your sweet little pussy does, don't they, butterfly?"

"Yes, yes," I cried, and he pinched them tight, making me orgasm again on shaky legs.

Before I'd had time to calm down, he dropped a pillow on the floor and pushed me to my knees.

As he pulled down his shorts, I stared. He wasn't wearing boxers underneath, and his cock was hard and huge. I'd never seen a cock before, much less his. It was easily eight, maybe nine inches, and almost as thick as my wrist. It wept at the almost purple tip.

"Kiss it," he ordered, and even though I suddenly felt shy, I did.

He groaned.

"Put your mouth around it, baby," he crooned, and curious, I did, giving it an experimental suck.

"Yes, fuck, yes. More. Wrap your lips around my cock and bob your head. Watch your teeth."

I did what he told me to, getting used to the way my mouth had to stretch around his girth, careful to keep my teeth away from his velvet hard length, licking him up and down as I tried bobbing and sucking.

He thrust his hips forward suddenly, his cock filling my airway passage, and I briefly choked.

"I'm sorry, butterfly, I'm sorry," he apologized, brushing my hair back from my face and gathering it into a ponytail. "Daddy doesn't want to hurt you, but he needs to feel that tight little throat swallow around his fat cock. Can you do that for me?"

I nodded, my mouth still full of him. Slowly, he pushed forward, his grip on my hair tightening. He hit the back of my throat and I panicked, pushing at his legs.

"Shh, shhh, you're okay," he crooned. "Breathe in through your nose. That's it. Just a little bit further."

He kept pushing until he slipped into my throat.

"Fuck, fuck, fuck, fuck," he chanted. "Daddy's going to come down this little throat, and then Daddy's going to get hard again and come in his virgin pussy."

Distantly, I realized he'd claimed ownership over my pussy again. Over me. But this time?

This time I wanted it. I hummed my agreement, and he groaned.

"I'm going to start fucking this throat and I want you to start rubbing that little clit for me at the same time. You're going to come when I do, butterfly."

I touched myself like he told me to. I was so much wetter than I'd been, and I cried out at the feel of my fingers, moaning around his cock.

"Fuuuuuck," he growled, and there went that response again, because at that growl, I came with a cry—and so did he, shooting his come deep down my throat and into my belly.

He withdrew, caressing my head as he did.

"Good, good girl," he said with a groan, lifting me up off the floor and sitting further back on my bed, cradling me in his lap. "You were so good to take me so deep." He caressed my hair, sighing. He was still hard under my ass, and I wiggled around on top of him.

He laughed. "I'm hurting almost as much as you are, butterfly. But let's catch our breath for a second. I need to hold you."

He kissed my forehead, humming something familiar. The mystery of the tune grounded me, helping me find some sliver of sanity among the wreckage of my desire.

Was he singing *Mulan?*

"Did you learn Disney for me?" I asked, shock making me forget my lust for a second.

He kissed my forehead again, nuzzling my hair. "Butterfly, I'd learn how to pilot a rocket ship, if I thought it would make you happy."

Even in my sex-haze, the sweetness of his words hit their target: my heart. I melted against him, trailing small, soft kisses across his neck and chest before burrowing into him.

"I mean it," he added.

"I believe you," I sighed.

We were quiet for a bit as he held me, but the sex-haze was too powerful, and I began to squirm. As nice as this was, the lust that had been temporarily banked roared back with a rage, and I needed him.

"That bad still, huh?" he murmured. "Okay, butterfly. It's time."

"Thank god," I gasped, and he laughed again, kissing my hair.

Laying me back on the bed, he kneeled in front of me and spread my thighs, grabbing

his cock with one hand and lining it up with my wet and aching pussy.

"No going back after this," he warned me as he stroked my clit with his cock, making me writhe underneath him.

"Please, Mason..."

"What do you call me?" he growled.

"Please, Daddy, I need you."

"I know, baby. Daddy needs you, too. Daddy's needed you for a long, long time, and now he finally has you. Now, you're finally his."

And with that, he began to push his way into my pussy. I was so wet that it eased his path, but I was a virgin, and tight, and the stretch hurt. Having someone inside of me felt invasive and strange; having my stepbrother's cock inside me as he stared deep into my eyes was a revelation.

"You feel so fucking good," he told me, his eyes deep. "This sweet little pussy was made for Daddy, wasn't it?"

"Yes, Daddy," I agreed, moaning in the back of my throat as he kept pushing into me until he paused.

"Are you all the way in?"

He chuckled, leaning down to kiss my lips. "Not even close."

And with that, he pulled his hips back and thrust hard. I screamed as this time, he bottomed out inside me.

"Shh, butterfly, shh," he murmured, rubbing circles on my clit until I relaxed and blossomed under him. It felt so good, having him deep inside me, touching me, filling me and surrounding me. I'd never felt so turned on—or so cared for in my life, and if I weren't so consumed by him and by sex, I'd question the fact that it was my greatest tormentor who had somehow become my safest place to land.

Once I began moaning again, he began circling his hips, around and around, stirring something inside of me and making me tighten even more.

"Daddy," I gasped.

"Good, butterfly?"

"So good."

Taking that, he began thrusting in and out of me, slow and deep, building up a pace. He kept angling and reangling his hips, obviously looking for something until—

"Oh!" I cried out. He'd rubbed up something deep inside of me that made shivers wrack my whole body, it felt so good. It set off whatever had made me feel so desperate in the first place, and I felt my core tighten as I spiraled closer to orgasm again.

"No you don't," he said darkly. "You don't come this time until I do, or you'll take me over with you. Daddy's just getting started."

With that, he began to play with my clit, drawing small, barely there circles, holding my hip tight with his other hand as he shoved faster and harder into me, moving me up the bed with his thrusts.

"Daddy, I can't, I need to—"

"Not yet," he ordered. "You can wait. Fuck, I'm so close." He slowed down, stirring his hips again, making me desperate and terrified that he'd never come—and never let me come, either.

"Please, please Daddy, please, please, please," I begged. "I'll do anything."

"Anything?" his eyes flashed, and I felt like I was signing my soul over to the devil—but I didn't care.

"Anything," I promised.

"My good little butterfly," he groaned, pumping his hips again, fast and hard. I was screaming at this point, and the whole dorm could probably hear me, and I didn't care. "Daddy's conquered this pussy, hasn't he? Permanently claimed what was always his. I'm going to come and fill you up and stuff you full, aren't I? Tell Daddy you want him to treat you like his perfect little cumdumpster."

The words should have shamed me, but instead they set some deep, secret part of me free.

"Daddy, I want you to treat me like your perfect little cumdumpster, please fill me up, Daddy, please—"

"FUUUUUUUUUUCK!" he pumped his hips inside me in uncontrolled movement, and I felt jet after jet of his seed fill me up. He pinched my clit once—tight and fast, and with one final scream, I orgasmed right after him, blacking out from the overwhelming pleasure.

When I came to, he was still inside me, but he was holding me on his lap, kissing my neck and stroking my hair as he hummed again. His cock was still hard. Waves of after-shocks moved through me, and I clenched around him.

"More?" he chuckled.

I could only moan in response.

"I know, baby, I know," he said, kissing my forehead. "Let me hold you some more. I've wanted you in my arms for as long as I've known you, and I'm not passing up the chance now."

He rocked me in his lap, humming again.

I'd learn how to pilot a rocket ship, if I thought it would make you happy.

The sweetness of his earlier confession settled in me. I, too, settled, this time against him, feeling safe and cared for for the first time in a very, very long time.

But soon I was grinding on top of him, a whine low in my throat. "Daddy—"

"Yes, baby," he crooned, lifting me up and lowering me onto his hard length. I felt full and sore and so, so right, even though a distant part of me was crying out that this was wrong, wrong, wrong.

17

MASON

I was going to hell. And I didn't even fucking care.

Because if I was going to hell, I was dragging Leslie with me. Wherever I went, she was joining. That was non-negotiable. I'd have to buy two first class tickets, because here was the simple truth:

I'd just fucked my stepsister.

I'd taken—no—*stolen* her virginity from her.

And all I felt was satisfied.

I didn't think I was at the same sociopathic levels as Jack Feldman, but I also didn't feel any guilt over what I'd done, and that was more than mildly concerning. Still, I had zero regrets—not after fucking Leslie for hours, and certainly not now, with her safely asleep in my arms. Especially not when she let out a sigh and snuggled closer. I used to hate cuddling; with Leslie, I couldn't get enough of her soft sweetness. It made something go tight in my chest, then release.

Mine.

Although it couldn't be this simple. Sure, she was purring contentedly like a kitten, now, I'd just had the best sex of my life, and my balls had finally released what felt like a year's worth of come. But when Leslie woke up and the Vixen wore off, she'd realize what I'd done. Shame would swamp her, and anger, and I could lose her when I'd finally, finally gotten a taste of her.

A lesser man would be fucking terrified of the coming fallout.

I wasn't a lesser man.

I didn't know how to prevent the freak out. It was valid for her to be pissed that I'd taken the decision away from her, I recognized that much. I wasn't some dickwad who would lie to myself about whether or not I'd taken advantage of her. She hadn't truly consented to this. She wasn't at fault here; I was. I just didn't care. She shouldn't feel guilt; I couldn't. I was incapable of it.

It was the encroaching shame she'd feel that wasn't valid. She'd hate that she slept with her stepbrother, and I wasn't sure how to convince her that we hadn't done anything wrong—or at least she hadn't. That we could be together going forward. We were adults, and only related by marriage. Whatever our parents and society thought now, they'd get over it.

Part of me wanted to kidnap her, take her away somewhere, some deserted island where it was just the two of us and no one could get to her or convince her that being with me was a bad idea.

But I couldn't do that. For one thing, I didn't *have* a deserted island. For another, Leslie was the sort of butterfly that needed light, sunshine, and other people. I'd isolated her once; I wouldn't do it again. I didn't know where that left us, but I knew I wasn't letting her go.

Not a chance in hell.

I did, however, need to give her everything she could ever want to make up for my sins. She deserved that much.

I gently shook her awake. "Butterfly."

"Mmm?" she stretched, opening her beautiful brown eyes.

"Butterfly."

"What is it?"

"I need you to tell me something," I murmured.

"Tell you what? I'll tell you anything." She giggled.

Perfect. If I was ever gonna get her to tell me something that embarassed her, it was now, blissed out on orgasms and still under the influence.

"Tell me about your most secret, shameful fantasy," I said.

"You are," she sighed, no pause, no hesitation, and some unfamiliar organ in my chest started to ache.

My heart.

Fuck.

I loved her.

I *loved* her.

Jesus fucking Christ. Of course I loved her.

She sighed again, reminding me about my mission. I could've stopped—I wanted to stop, to bask in her response and my realization, but I jostled her again.

"Beyond that. What's something that makes those panties wet but also makes you think you need to talk to a priest?"

She laughed, sounding a little more coherent. "I'm Jewish, Mason. We don't have priests. Or confession."

"Butterfly."

Her face colored. "Okay, I have one fantasy...that the man I'm with forces me to fuck someone else."

I froze, and my heart no longer ached—it *burned.*

"Someone else?"

"Both of them, at once," she said dreamily. "And I have no choice but to do what he says..."

I wanted to punch a hole in the wall behind the bed, but that would ruin her peace, so I made myself stay calm. After inhaling and exhaling slowly, I asked, "And would this be a regular thing? Would there be a third in the relationship?"

"Noooooo..." she blinked. "I don't think so? No, not that." She sounded sure, and so I relaxed—slightly. "But it would prove that he trusted me, trusted in us...and that he was so proud of me, that he realized other men would want me. He'd keep me safe, but let me have that, too...no one's ever done anything like that for me before, and no one ever will..."

She trailed off, yawning.

"Go back to sleep," I said.

"Okay, Daddy," she agreed, and a moment later, she was dreaming again. Hopefully not about a second man.

Fuck.

I couldn't do it. Couldn't share her, no matter how much she wanted it, no matter how hot it might be. Every single cell in my body agreed. She was mine. No one else got to touch her.

But if that's what she wanted? It was my job to make her happy.

If I could learn fucking *Mulan*, could I learn to share?

The comparison made me laugh, disturbing Leslie, who murmured something in her sleep.

Mine.

I wrapped her tighter in my arms, leaning my head back against the wall, and shutting my eyes, letting myself imagine a perfect world where this was my life, fucking Leslie into submission every night and filling her with my come, protecting her whispered secrets, and then holding her in my arms as we slept. And in the morning, she'd smile that brilliant smile at me, filled with devotion, trust, and love.

It would happen. I would stop at nothing to make sure it did.

Even if I worried she'd hate me when she realized what I'd done.

It didn't take her long.

Sunlight streamed in through her window, blinding me. Next to me, Leslie stirred beneath my arms, groaning.

"My head hurts. Why does my head hurt so much?"

"I'm sorry, butterfly," I said, kissing her forehead. "It's my fault. I'll get you ibuprofen and water."

She stilled in my arms.

"Mason?"

I stilled, too.

"Yes," I said cautiously.

"Oh god, it wasn't a dream."

She sat up, swatting at my arm and wrenching away. I fisted my hands, forcing myself not to reach for her and pull her back where she was safe and undoubtedly mine. I would give her a few minutes to process.

A minute.

Fuck that. She got five seconds and then she was going right back where I wanted her.

"Mason, you can't be here. What if someone finds us? I don't know why I did what I did last night, I felt like I was out of my mind with lust, like I was drugged, and I fucked you and you fucked me, all night long, I gave you my *virginity*, and you're my stepbrother and you *hate me!* God, did we even lock the door last night? What if someone knows? What if they tell our parents? Why did I do that? How *could* I do that?"

She was hyperventilating. Alarmed, I grabbed her hand. "Breathe."

She ripped it away. "I need you to go, Mason. Now. Please, I am begging you. I don't know how this happened, but you need to leave before something... irrevocable happens."

This time, I needed to breathe, before I got angry. Irrevocable? Like taking her virginity, fucking her without a condom, coming inside her? We'd crossed the point of no return already. I was considering *sharing* her, for fuck's sake.

I took a deep breath, regulating my temper. I'd known she'd feel this way, and it was my job to calm her down, take the blame, and convince her this was right.

But first I needed to make sure she didn't run. I pushed her down and rolled over her, lifting myself in a push up so she was trapped underneath my body. My cock, which should've been worn out, started hardening, reminding me we liked this position.

"I'll tell you how this happened," I said, gentle and easy, not wanting to spook her. "I put Vixen in your coffee yesterday morning, and it unleashed all your inner desire."

"Vixen?" She gaped at me. "You mean that drug they're talking about on the news? The aphrodisiac?"

"That's the one."

She shoved at me, but I didn't budge. "You drugged me? How fucking dare you."

"You're right. But I'm not sorry. It was the only way to get us here, butterfly. Tell me, do you regret it? Truly?"

She glared at me. "You took my virginity, and I wasn't even in my right mind. Do you really think I don't regret it?"

Damn. I knew it had been coming, but it still stung.

I lowered myself, kissing her unwilling lips, coaxing them until she gasped and they parted for me, saying everything I couldn't say. Not yet.

My erection strained between us as I smothered her "regret" with my affection, passion, and desire for her.

"The drug left your system hours ago," I told her. "So then why did you kiss me back?"

"That's not fair,' she protested. "You like, made me imprint on you, or some shit."

"Huh?"

"Never mind, it's a *Twilight* thing," she grumbled.

I brushed that shit off. Bella should've picked the werewolf kid, anyway.

"I'll make this up to you, I promise." For the rest of our lives, if I had to. "Starting with you staying in bed while I get you water and ibuprofen. Let me take care of you, butterfly."

"I don't want you to take care of me. I want you *gone.*"

"And I want to hold you some more," I said easily. Or as easily as I could.

"You're not touching me ever again."

"That's not what you wanted last night."

"Well, I don't think last night counts if I was *drugged.* I was out of my mind horny, I can't be blamed for this."

"Who the hell is talking about blame? What are you really saying here, butterfly?"

"I'm saying that this can't happen again. And that you need to leave, now."

"No."

"Leave, or I call our parents."

I couldn't let her do that. When they found out about us,

we needed to be a solid, unwavering unit, not at war. If Leslie told her mom, she'd never trust me. My father already barely trusted me. And they'd never believe we had a loving, consenting relationship—which was fair, given the current circumstances. But we would, one day.

I just needed to get her over this hurdle.

"Butterfly, you aren't going to do that. You aren't going to tell your mommy you fucked her darling stepson on drugs. How do you think she'll respond?"

Leslie glared at me. It had been the wrong thing to say. "Get. Out."

Sighing, I grabbed my jeans and t-shirt, dressing with my back to her so she couldn't see my face. I could hear her breathing behind me, heavily. If she was crying...

She was. And when she saw me looking at her, she wiped angrily at her face.

"Leave."

"I'm not leaving while you're this upset," I told her as I approached her. "It's my job as your Daddy to see to your needs—all of them."

"You aren't my Daddy," she countered.

"That's not what you were saying last night."

She looked at me. "Are you legitimately insane?"

I shrugged. "Maybe."

She shook this off, continuing. "You drugged me last night. *You*. Anything I said, I wasn't in my right mind."

I approached her, pulling her into my arms. She resisted, but I didn't let her, tightening my hold on her until her tears wet my shirt. "The Vixen made you out of your mind with lust, but I think you can admit it didn't make you say anything. You called me Daddy in the stacks, remember?"

She bit me in retaliation. I laughed. I loved her fire.

But I needed her to admit to the truth, so I leaned back,

lifting her chin so she had to look me in the eyes. The tears made hers sparkle, and all I wanted was to kiss her.

Focus, Mason.

"I know you're ashamed of what happened, so you're trying to backtrack. And you aren't to blame for this—I accept responsibility. But you're also ashamed because we're stepsiblings, and that shouldn't stop you. Let yourself want what you want without so much internal judgment. We'll both be happier."

She shoved me away.

"Leave. *Please*," she begged. "I need to think."

Sighing, I released her. Hovering would just make her want to push me away more. I needed to retreat and restrategize. My absence would make her miss me, force her to come to me. It was the right next step, even though I hated everything about it.

I turned toward the door, stopping to say, "It's too late to turn back from this, butterfly. I told you last night, no take backs. You want irrevocable? This became irrevocable the moment I saw you dancing at our parents' wedding."

I left her staring at me, eyes round and wet. It took everything in me not to turn back, pull her into my arms, and never let her go.

18

LESLIE

I was a mess. More than usual, even.

It had been a week since I'd seen Mason, and even though I was pissed at him, I couldn't stop dreaming about the fucking asshole. Couldn't stop thinking about how he'd felt inside me, urging me toward bliss I couldn't have imagined. I hated him, but I wanted that feeling back, and I couldn't get there with my own hand.

It was more than the sex. I'd played the *Mulan* soundtrack over and over, like it would bring back that feeling of safety and joy I'd had when he'd hummed "A Girl Worth Fighting For" to me in his low, husky baritone.

It didn't. He'd ruined Disney for me.

My phone taunted me every night. I'd open the text message between us, only to close it and throw my phone across my bed as if it had burned me. I'd expected him to text me, or find me, or something, but it was like he'd actually listened when I'd told him to stay away.

And I missed the stupid fucker.

Maybe he had lied. Maybe I didn't matter to him at all.

And wasn't that a mind-fuck, realizing that I wanted to matter to him, after everything he'd done?

I kept trying to tell myself it was for the best. There was no way I could have a relationship with someone so cruel. And I couldn't be with my stepbrother, it would kill my mother, his father, and we'd never be able to show our faces at home. It was too embarrassing, shameful even.

So then why did I want it so badly? I lay awake at night in bed, thinking of the way he'd felt, around me, inside me, on top of me, and I wanted him back. I tried to get off, but all I could see was him, and it was like now that my pussy had had the real thing, she didn't want my hand as a consolation prize.

I wanted Mason. But I couldn't have him, or be with him, and it was pretty obvious that even though he was pissed at me, he was fine with moving on and going back to torturing me.

I was not looking forward to class this morning, either, knowing he'd be there, but maybe it would be okay if he sat somewhere else and ignored me.

I stumbled my way into the bathroom, rubbing the sleep out of my eyes. I didn't even have time for a shower, and I hoped my hair wouldn't look too awful if I pulled it into a top knot.

"You look wrecked," Lucy greeted me in front of the sinks, same as last time.

"I feel wrecked," I told her, handing her her shower caddie. "Do I want to know how you've been brushing your teeth?"

She waved me off. "I have an extra. Besides, we're focusing on you. Does the feeling wrecked have anything to do with Mr. Hottie who left your room the other morning? I saw what happened in the cafeteria the other day. That was brutal." She shuddered in commiseration.

"It was. Are you trying to rub it in my face?" I didn't have the time or energy for coy pleasantries today.

She put her hands up. "Hey, hey, I'm on your side. I want to be your friend. I was observing that things looked bad between the two of you. I'm sorry."

I sighed. "It's not bad... or it is bad...it's confusing. I'm confused."

"Tell me about it."

"I'm running late to class, and besides..." I trailed off. I desperately needed a friend to talk to, but telling a stranger I'd just lost my virginity to my stepbrother was not on the list of things I wanted to do today, or ever.

"How about we hang out in my room later, drink tequila, and you can tell me what's going on? I'm telling you, I'm deeply curious. Whatever it is, it looks messy and you probably need someone to vent to so we can swear off men forever together, right?"

I laughed, then glanced at my phone. "Shit, I've got to go." I brushed my teeth, threw my hair up into something resembling a top knot, and ran out of the bathroom.

"Room 309! Don't forget!" she called after me.

I STOPPED AT THE CAFETERIA TO GRAB A QUICK BREAKFAST, alone, like I had for the past week. And, just like I had for the past week, I could barely chew and swallow a banana, much less anything more substantial. Between the anxiety from Mason's silence, and the shame that swirled in my head every morning after dreaming about him the night before, I felt too nauseous to be able to eat. It was affecting my energy and mood and I just wanted to curl up in a ball and hide under the covers.

That said, I forced myself to eat a banana and two bites of toast. As I chewed, I felt eyes on my back. I turned. Mason sat with Emory and his other friends. Emily was nowhere in sight. His intense, almost warm look turned into a glare as he took in my cafeteria tray.

Yeah, that was it. If he wasn't going to talk to me but just glare at me from afar, for no discernible reason, then I was getting out of here. Besides, I didn't want to be late for our class.

I FOUND AN EMPTY ROW OF SEATS, WANTING TO BE ALONE WITH my thoughts. No luck; Dan joined me immediately.

"You okay?" he asked, his brow furrowed.

I pasted a smile on my face. "Fine!" I chirped.

"Okay...." he said, clearly not believing me. "By the way, your stepbrother is watching us."

Of course he was.

My phone buzzed.

I expected it to be something along the lines of... *stop talking to other men*, so I was surprised when it read, *Are you eating?*

My practically empty stomach churned. He saw me too clearly.

I ignored the text, focusing on what Professor Evans was saying about *The Scarlet Letter*—specifically the way female desire was both demonized, and how women were equally infantilized and vilified when it came to sex...at least in the book.

I knew something about that, didn't I? I'd had no agency

the other night, and I felt vilified for how much I wanted Mason. Although, who was vilifying me? Mason certainly wasn't ...In fact, he'd done the opposite: taking responsibility for what had happened the night he drugged me, demanding I not shame myself for wanting him or for what was happening between us.

I was vilifying *myself*.

And while he'd completely taken away my choice that night, and I couldn't control the fact that I wanted him, I got to decide what I did next.

I didn't have an answer to that, and unfortunately as class went on, I began to feel weak and had a harder time focusing on the discussion. I didn't even notice when Professor Evans dismissed the class.

"Ms. Berger?" Professor Evans stood over me, a worried expression on her young face.

"I'm okay," I said.

"You don't seem okay."

"I'm fine," I said. "Just need to get home. Sorry I was so quiet in...class today. Sleeping poorly."

"Mmhmm," she said. "I think—"

"I've got this," a low voice said. "Leslie, what's going on?"

Mason crouched next to my desk, a hand on my thigh as he looked into my eyes.

"I'm fine," I said again, stronger this time. "I need to go, though."

"Okay, then stand up," he said. "Let's see how 'fine' you are."

He and the professor exchanged a look, and then he stood and both backed up to let me up. I slid out from my desk and I must have risen too quickly because I immediately felt dizzy and stumbled. And I would've fallen, if it weren't for Mason. The moment I lost my balance, he was there, scooping me up into his arms.

"You don't have to carry me," I protested weakly, even as I was distracted by the safety of his strong arms. I didn't trust him, but I knew he'd die before he'd drop me.

That didn't make him any less of a bossy asshole.

"You aren't in a position to tell me what to do," he told me firmly. "You obviously can't walk right now, probably because you barely ate this morning."

"Try the past week," I muttered.

He growled. "We'll be talking about that." To the professor he said, "Can you hand me her bag? I'm going to get her home and get some food in her. Make sure she rests."

"Of course." Professor Evans grabbed up my bag and handed it to Mason, who slung it over his shoulder like it was nothing. "Will you let me know how she's doing?"

"I'm fine," I said again, squirming.

He squeezed my thigh in reprimand. "I'll keep you updated," he told her.

"Feel better, Ms. Berger," Professor Evans said, winking at me.

And with that, he carried me out of the classroom and building, ignoring the eyes and whispers on us.

"This is embarrassing," I complained.

"You should think of that the next time you decide to go on a hunger strike," he said as he walked, being careful not to jostle me. "Besides, I like having you in my arms—but next time it better be under better circumstances."

"What, she can't even walk on her own two feet now?" I heard a high female voice ask, and craned my neck.

And I'll admit, I took some satisfaction in seeing Emily

with a hand on her hip, looking hugely put out by Mason carrying me.

Mason glared at her. "Emily, fuck the hell off." Ignoring her gasp of outrage, he lifted me higher in his arms and placing a light kiss on my forehead. "You can close your eyes, butterfly. You're safe...for now."

"What's that supposed to mean?" I yawned, suddenly feeling very tired.

"It means that bad girls who don't take care of themselves get punished by their Daddy. Part of the whole care and protect package. Now shhh, I've got you."

The words were oddly comforting, even as they spread heat through my abdomen. But the dizziness and exhaustion overwhelmed me, and as unbelievable as it sounds, I fell asleep in his arms as he carried me home.

19

MASON

This was my fault.

I'd thought leaving Leslie alone was the right idea. She was *supposed* to miss me and come to me, of her own volition. I wanted to give her the choice, and I'd truly—stupidly—believed she would. I hadn't taken into account how stubborn she was, how angry she'd been about my drugging her, and, mostly, how her shame would control her. And I had completely overlooked the possibility that she'd punish herself by not eating. I'd focused on hockey practice to keep myself from giving in and going to her. I wanted to rage at myself; stand in the middle of the rink without protective gear and let every player hit puck after puck at my head. Being mine meant she was my responsibility, and I'd fallen down on the job.

But I was fixing it now.

I carried her across campus to my building, climbing up the stairs with her still in my arms and unlocking the door to my suite. For once, no one else was home, so I took her into my bedroom and carefully placed her on my bed. She immediately curled on her side, her shiny black hair spreading out over the pillow. Satisfaction filled me, seeing her exactly where she belonged, on my bed, in my room, fully ensconced in my life. Sitting beside her, I brushed her hair off her forehead, leaning in to kiss her hair, smelling that flowers and sunshine scent that belonged to her and her alone. It had quickly become my favorite smell.

Reluctantly, I rose and went to the kitchen. I never cooked—I wasn't great at it, and also, I'd never had to. But Emory's private chef wasn't going to be here for a few hours, and I wanted to make sure my butterfly had food she'd actually want to eat. Luckily, I'd watched Leslie closely enough to know what her favorite foods were: blackened chicken fettuccine alfredo, strawberry and goat cheese salad, and a certain brand of peach ice cream. We didn't have the ingredients for most of it, so I put in an order on the grocery delivery app. I had to order from three different grocery stores—one didn't have blackened seasoning, and neither of the first two had the right peach ice cream so I had to order from a specialty store—but nothing was too much for Leslie. I not only owed her, but I wanted her to be happy.

And I already knew the only thing more satisfying than seeing her asleep on my bed, would be seeing her eating the food I'd made for her.

I couldn't wait.

EMORY AND MATT WERE HOME BY THE TIME THE GROCERIES arrived, so they were there to heckle me through three botched attempts before I got the pasta right and moved onto the salad.

"Man, you must really like this girl," Matt commented from the couch.

"Love her," I corrected quietly, eyes on my bedroom.

I'd checked on Leslie a few times, but she was absolutely wiped, sleeping through the entire thing—even when I'd burned the chicken the second time and set off the smoke detector. She was still asleep, which was good—I wasn't ready for her to know how I felt.

I'd loved her a long time. Maybe I'd loved her from the first moment I'd seen her, dancing at our parents' wedding. The realization had snuck up on me before dropping like a bomb that night I'd finally fucked her, but saying it out loud felt right. It was more true than anything I'd ever acknowledged in my life, and unlike when we first met, it no longer scared me.

I threw the salad together as best I could, but the goat cheese was mushed together and stuck to the greens.

"What am I doing wrong?" I said, staring in consternation at the stupid salad.

Emory was laughing hysterically. "Dude, you got the wrong kind of goat cheese."

I ran a hand through my hair—probably leaving bits of goat cheese residue in the strands. *Fuck.* "There's more than one kind of goat cheese?"

"You need to get the crumbled kind, jackass," Matt pointed out, unhelpfully.

"You're the jackass, jackass," I retorted half-heartedly.

Damn it.

"It'll taste the same," Emory pointed out.

Sighing, I poured some salad dressing on top, fixed the food on a plate, laid it all out on a tray, plucked a flower out of the bouquet I'd bought along with the groceries and put it in a glass, and carried it all into the bedroom.

"Good luck! Hope you don't give her food poisoning," Matt said.

"Shut up, you idiot, he's finally doing the right thing for once," Emory said, smacking him.

Ignoring them, I entered the now dark bedroom. I walked over to the bed, placing the tray on the nightstand, and leaned down to kiss Leslie. "Wake up, sleeping beauty," I murmured.

She yawned, opening her eyes. "Mason? Where am I?"

"My place," I told her.

She struggled to sit up. I helped her, propping pillows behind her. She swatted my hands away.

"I can do it. I'm not helpless, you know. I was just tired, and hungry." Then she sniffed the air. "Is that blackened chicken alfredo?"

"It is, and goat cheese strawberry salad. And there's peach ice cream in the freezer for dessert."

"Those are my favorite foods. How did you know?"

I smiled at her. "The same way I knew how you like your coffee. I know everything about you. I've majored in Leslie Berger, don't you know?" The truth was, I'd asked her mother a number of questions about Leslie before I left for Tabb, but I wasn't about to bring Anna up in conversation; the reminder that we were related by marriage wouldn't get me very far.

Before she could respond, I picked up the glass of water. "Thirsty?"

She nodded. I held the glass to her lips, and after some hesitation, she drank from it. I tried not to get distracted by the way her throat worked, remembering how it felt when she'd swallowed around my cock. It wasn't the right time; that could come later.

When she was finished, she tapped my arm and I lowered the glass to the tray. "Did you...make it yourself?"

I nodded. "I did."

"I didn't know you cooked."

"I don't."

She processed this. Feeling unfamiliarly awkward, I said, "I kind of fucked up the salad, though. Apparently I used the wrong kind of goat cheese."

This, of all things, made her smile. "Thank you, Mace," she said, and even though I'd hated being called Mace in the past, the sweet way she said it made my chest squeeze. "But I'm not hungry."

Oh no, that wasn't going to fly. "Butterfly, you need to eat."

"I can't, I'm too anxious," she admitted, looking away.

I stroked a hand through her hair, turning her face back to mine. "Why?"

Her eyes went wet with tears. "Because of you," she whispered.

Ah, fuck.

"Because I drugged you?"

She nodded.

"And took your virginity?"

She nodded again.

"And was cruel to you for so long?"

"Yes. I don't know what's real, and what isn't. I'm so angry at you for what you did, but I..."

"Want me at the same time," I said, knowingly.

"...Yes."

I ran a finger down her cheek. "It's okay, butterfly. Remember what I told you—what happened that night isn't your fault, it's mine. I'm not going to apologize for it, because it was the best night of my life, and I wouldn't trade it for anything. But I am sorry for making you so anxious you couldn't eat. It won't happen again. But you need to eat. Can you eat, for Daddy?"

"It was the best night of your life?" She was still stuck on that.

"Yes, butterfly. Nothing compares. Nothing." My voice was fierce.

"Okay." She reached for the fork, but I grabbed it from her.

"No, Daddy's going to feed you," I told her, spinning pasta around the fork and holding it up to her lips.

After a moment, she opened her mouth and let me feed her. Each time she put her lips around the tines and accepted the food from me, my cock got harder. It wasn't hard to picture doing this another time, with her in my lap, my cock deep inside her as she took food from me.

Along with my hard cock, my heart felt full. Deeply satisfied, just like I'd known it would. She was eating the food I'd bought for her, made for her, and now was feeding her directly. It settled something in me I hadn't realized had felt off until now. This was my purpose. This was what I was supposed to be doing with my life—taking care of her. It was all I wanted, and it was almost within reach.

After chewing, she said, "Mace, I have a question for you."

"Go for it."

"This summer...was taking naked pictures of me your idea?"

I'd been waiting for this. "No. But it was my fault. I hadn't realized how jealous Tiffanie was. I should've. None of those pictures made it online, by the way. I made everyone delete all of them off their phones. And I never spoke to her again."

She nodded. "I knew the photos didn't make it online. But why didn't you tell me at the time?"

I sighed, taking her hand in mine. It was so small, so

delicate. Everything about her was delicate. "I couldn't let on that it pissed me off, or those assholes would have done worse. And I was so angry at you, I didn't want to tell you. Tried to tell myself that you leaving was the right thing."

"Why were you so angry?"

I stabbed some salad with the fork and brought it to her lips. She took it easily, chewing and swallowing. Color had returned to her cheeks, and she seemed more like herself. Relief swamped me.

"Mason."

"Call me Mace again," I urged.

"Mace."

"I was angry at you, butterfly. You'd made me want things I'd never wanted before, and it felt like those things were out of reach. I didn't know who to blame, so I blamed you. It made it easier to keep you at a distance."

She swallowed. "What changed?"

"It wasn't easier when you left. It was worse. I swore to myself I'd never let you leave again. I mean that. You're mine now. You've been mine since before I slid deep inside that perfect pussy and took your virginity. Before the first time I kissed you. Before that night in the pool. Before we even met for the first time. You've been mine since before you were born. You were made for me, and if you don't see that now, you will. I promise."

She didn't say anything for a moment, then finally: "How do you know?

This time, I was the one who had to swallow. My whole mouth felt like sawdust; I never talked about this out loud.

"You know my mom died, right?"

"Yeah. I'm sorry, Mason." She squeezed my hand, and the unexpected gesture of support made that sawdust taste disappear.

"She had Marfan syndrome. It's this rare degenerative disease, it affects your connective tissues so your body fails, and then your eyes." I swallowed again, shutting my own eyes. "I had to sit there and watch as my mom lost mobility, then her eyesight, getting sicker and sicker and weaker and weaker, until her heart finally gave out."

"Oh, Mason." She squeezed my hand again, her eyes filling with tears. "That's horrible, I'm sorry."

"You know the worst thing? Besides losing the person who loved you most in the world. My dad kind of died, too. All I had left was hockey. It never let me down, it was always there for me, so I devoted myself to it and stayed cold to everything and everyone else. When your mom came around, I was so fucking pissed that anyone could replace her, but it wasn't your mom's fault. She makes my dad happy. That's a good thing." And she'd brought me Leslie, which was the best thing.

Leslie sighed, running her thumb in circles over my palm. "Feeling like you've been replaced *sucks.*"

I stilled, waiting for her to tell me about her own wounds.

"My dad...you know how soap operas always have these men who have a second family?" She bit her lip, and I silently urged her to continue, to trust me. "Well, my dad is one of those men, except *we* were the second family. My mom was never married to him, but she didn't realize that she was his side piece."

"Oh, butterfly."

She shrugged. "He was always out of town for work, never around. I thought he did something *so important.* I was *proud* of him. Until we found out. And it wasn't like he loved us more; when Mom confronted him, he went back to his wife and kids. And I've always wondered why we weren't enough for him. Why we weren't worthy of him."

She shook her head, and anger at her pain filled me.

I spoke. "Two things. First: I hate that you've been hurt, but no one will ever hurt you again." Except maybe me, but I'd make sure I'd only hurt her in ways now that set up her happiness later. "Second: I'll kill him."

She laughed. "Cute. I appreciate the—"

"No, butterfly," I interrupted. "I mean it. Anyone who hurts you doesn't deserve to breathe."

She stilled, her thumb pausing in its circles. "Mason, I don't want that. I don't like violence, and I don't want you hurting anyone—not even for me."

I knew she'd feel that way, but I didn't give a fuck.

"It's not up for discussion, Leslie."

"Mason, I mean it." She lifted her hand, placing it on my cheek. "I don't know what this is between us, if it can be anything—"

"It's everything," I interrupted her.

She gasped, her eyes going wide. "It can't be."

"I'm not arguing about this, butterfly. You're mine."

Her voice was quiet when she said, "If you hurt someone —even for me—then I'm gone."

I digested this. I wouldn't kill her father then, as much as it pained me. As for anyone else? Well, what Leslie didn't know wouldn't hurt *her*.

As for any man who threatened her...

"Okay," I said, then changed the subject. "There's peach ice cream for you."

"Peach ice cream?" She shook her head, cracking a smile. "I'm too full to eat it, which sucks."

"Alright, you can have it later. It's time for your punishment."

"My...what?"

"You heard me. You're feeling better now, you got rest. Now you're going to learn that you have to take care of yourself, or you'll have Daddy to answer to."

"But..."

I shook my head. "No buts. Time to stand up, strip and bend over the bed like a good girl."

20

LESLIE

He couldn't be serious.

We'd just confessed our deep pain to each other, gotten really vulnerable. I expected sex after, sure, but this? There was no way he actually believed I'd let him *spank* me. I was not a child, or like, his submissive in a dirty romance novel or something. Sure, I had called him Daddy a few times, but that didn't give him permission to *punish* me.

Except as I gaped at him, he didn't look like he was kidding. His face was stern, his eyes were hot. And—I glanced down—his cock was hard. And if Mason had proven anything to me, it was that it didn't matter if I gave him permission. If he wanted it, he'd take it.

And I hated it, but just knowing that about him made me soak my panties.

"Strip, Leslie," he said, his voice quiet but unyielding.

"And what happens if I don't?"

His voice was gruff. Low. "Then I make you. And I double your punishment."

Well, that didn't sound fun.

So I stood and pulled my shirt over my head, then unbuttoned and wiggled out of my shorts. I stood in front of him, fisting my hands at my sides in order not to hide myself from his gaze. He'd seen me naked before, anyway.

"Underwear, too."

Annoyed at the slight tremble in my hands, I undid my bra and let it fall to the floor, then lowered my panties. And apparently it didn't matter that Mason had seen me naked before. Between the heat of his gaze on me and the way he growled "beautiful" under his breath as he scanned my body up and down, rubbing a hand over his cock, this time felt like the first time. I'd never been more afraid and I'd never felt more needy.

But he wasn't going to touch me the way I wanted.

"Bend over."

I hesitated. There was a fork in this road, and if I followed this path, I wasn't sure where it led, but I knew it was somewhere intense and terrifying. But if I followed the other, it would lead me away from Mason, and I knew I didn't want that anymore. He'd carried me all the way across campus. Brought me to his home. Fed me all my favorite foods—made them himself!—just to make sure I ate. Told me about how his mom had died, and how much it hard hurt him. And I'd been right: The photos this summer hadn't been his idea. I knew I wanted him, physically. Maybe, just maybe, I wanted him for more than that.

Even if that meant bending over his bed and letting him rain terror down on my ass. If he wanted to play Daddy, then I was going to let him.

So I slowly bent over, pushing my ass out toward him and burying my head in the comforter. It smelled like

Mason: like ocean spray and oranges and danger. The smell instantly calmed me, even as it aroused me.

"Good, good girl," he praised behind me, running a big, warm hand over my left ass cheek, then my right. "Count."

Then, without any further warning, he slapped my right ass cheek—hard.

"Hey!" I complained.

"That doesn't sound like counting. Try again."

He smacked my left ass cheek that time—even harder.

"One," I grumbled.

He smacked me a third time. "One, who?"

Oh, *god.* The realization that that was what he wanted from me made the heat from his spanks slide down between my cheeks and around to my clit.

"One, Daddy," I said, my voice breathy.

"That's right," he said, his voice warm and soothing in its praise. "That's exactly what you call me, because I'm taking care of my girl right now, aren't I? Punishing her, so she knows how to behave better—and take better care of herself, too."

With that, he smacked my ass again.

"Two," I squeaked.

Smack.

Smack.

Slap.

"Three, Daddy."

"Four, Daddy."

"Five, Daddy."

The spanking continued, the heat and pain growing, morphing. I didn't know how many times he was going to spank me. He hadn't told me. I did know that I was getting so wet from it, I was worried I'd drip all over his comforter or floor. And I was so turned on, I might come from this alone. An orgasm loomed in the distance, like a far off wave from shore.

He paused, sliding his hand between my thighs and brushing his fingers over my pussy.

"Oh, you good girl, you like this, don't you? Taste how wet you are." He lifted his fingers away from me, and then they were painting my own wetness on my lips and forcing their way into my mouth. I almost choked on them, and on my own taste—salty and sweet and unfamiliar. My whole body went red with embarrassment....and desire.

The wave rolled closer.

He pulled his fingers away. Then:

Slap!

Slap!

Slap!

These were delivered to the underside of my ass.

"Six. Seven. Eight, Daddy."

The wave grew closer still. I was so close. All I had to do was tip my hips forward and rub my pussy against the bed and I would come. I would—

His hands on my hips stilled me. "You get to come when I say so, butterfly. For now, take your punishment."

"But how much more?!" I cried. "I don't think I can hold off."

"You can. You will. Just two more and you're done with your punishment."

Smack. Nine. On the inside of my thigh. The orgasm loomed over me.

"Butterfly?"

"Nine, Daddy, sorry."

He didn't say anything, and I clenched everything in anticipation of the last spank—completely shocked when he brought his hand around to my front. Was he going to get me off instead?

The burn from his last spank—right on my pussy—told me otherwise.

"Ten, Daddy!" I screamed, barely holding off from coming.

"Good girl, you took your punishment so well," he said, as I shook from the effort of staving off the approaching orgasm. It was so close I could taste it.

"Please, Daddy," I begged.

"Mmm. Please, what?"

"Please, let me come..."

"Good girl," he praised. "My good little butterfly. She gets exactly what she needs. Daddy will always give you what you need. Wait here. And do not touch yourself."

I waited as Mason disappeared out of his room, closing the door softly behind him and locking it. The pleasure began to dissipate and I breathed more easily, relieved and disappointed. Was he done with me?

When he returned with a pint of peaches and cream ice cream, something in my heart went squishy. I didn't even know you could get my favorite ice cream on campus.

"Mason, thank you, but I'm not hungry," I said again.

"You'll have a little," he said.

"Mason..."

But he was flipping me over onto my back, kneeling down in front of me, dragging me down the bed by my thighs before throwing both my legs over his shoulders. Before I could say anything, he'd spooned up some ice cream and reached his hand up so the spoon brushed my lips. I couldn't help myself; I opened my mouth to savor my favorite treat.

"Good girl."

His hand disappeared, and as I swallowed the sweet, tangy, smooth ice cream, something cold, wet, and sticky hit my breasts. I jumped.

"What?"

"It's my turn for dessert," he growled, and then his mouth enveloped my left breast. He began swirling his tongue around my nipple and the combination of cold ice cream and his hot mouth brought the orgasm back. He moved his mouth to my right breast, and when he licked me there, there was more cold ice cream beneath his hot mouth.

I moaned, writhing beneath him, as he trailed ice cream down my ribcage to my belly button to my right hip, his tongue following. As he licked and sucked my skin, I discovered new erogenous zones I'd never known existed: my left lower rib, the area right under my belly button, my hip bone. Pausing, he spooned more ice cream into my mouth. I swallowed down the taste of fresh peaches and cream, the silky sweetness a tease on my tongue as Mason continued to tease me, making his way from my hip bone to my pussy, before he swirled circles around my clit with his tongue.

I screamed as the orgasm broke over me like a tidal wave. Screamed again as he began licking and sucking and biting, not relenting, the orgasm continuing as it sucked me down, down, down beneath the surface. It was so intense, so brilliantly, painfully pleasurable, I wasn't sure I'd ever make it out.

Finally, he stopped, placing soft kisses above my mound and on my thighs as he rose to his feet and pulled me into his arms.

"I think that's my favorite dessert now," he commented.

"What, peaches and cream ice cream?" I asked shakily.

"No, Daddy's pussy," he corrected me. "Although if I could make an ice cream that tasted like you, I would. I'd never share it though, just keep it to myself. I'd have to make you come over and over and over again and package it up, leave it in the freezer for whenever I was hungry." He looked at me, considering.

Everything in me went tight all over at the thought. He chuckled.

"Some other time."

He stroked my back for a bit, both of us silent, me on his lap, him surrounding, big, and hard, and perfect. I felt safe and protected in a way I never had before, which was funny, since he was the one who I'd once needed protection from.

And maybe still did.

He'd spanked me, without my permission.

And you liked it, my inner voice pointed out.

"What was that thought?" he asked.

"What do you mean?"

"You just stiffened up and went beet red. Something upset you. What was it?"

I shook my head. "I don't want to talk about it."

"Not an option," he told me sternly. "It's not just your body that's mine. All of you is mine. What's in here," he placed his hand at my heart, "and what's in here," he tapped my forehead.

"You can't just...claim me like that."

He ignored me. "Are you embarrassed because you liked your spanking?"

I didn't respond. That told him enough.

"Why? We both enjoyed it. It didn't hurt anyone. You know I've done worse, so why are *you* embarrassed?"

How could I explain that, as a recent virgin, all of this

was new to me? Or that even if I'd gotten off to fantasies of that sort of treatment in the past, the reality was much more intense, and made me question everything about myself? And that didn't even take into account my *other* fantasy. I doubted Mason would be interested in sharing me.

"I'm not a doormat," I told him instead.

"I know you aren't. If you were, I wouldn't want you," he said easily. "But letting me take you in hand, into my care—letting me punish you when you do badly in order to help you do better for yourself in the future—that's not you being a doormat. That's you learning to trust me."

"And you think it's that easy for me to trust you, after all you've done?"

He sighed. "No. But I have faith you'll get there."

"Why?"

"Because you not getting there with me isn't an option. I'll do everything I need to, wait for as long as I have to, to make sure you give all of yourself to me. I'm not a quitter, and I'm not easily defeated. You're mine, butterfly, and I'm yours. Do us both a favor and realize it, and Daddy will reward you."

I started to rise from the bed.

"Where do you think you're going?"

"Back to my dorm. I need to think."

"You're staying here until I'm sure you're capable of taking care of yourself," he said darkly. "I want you here for the weekend, and likely longer."

"Mason!"

"Mace."

"Mace." I stroked his face. "Let me go home."

"No." He kissed my hand. "Nice attempt at manipulation, though."

"I learned from the best," I grumbled.

"See?" He laughed. "We were made for each other."

Maybe he was right. But it didn't matter, because we were stepsiblings. I wasn't ready to give him up, but I knew we had no future. Even if we were made for each other, we could never be together.

So why did that make my heart crack in two?

21

LESLIE

In the end, it took the entire weekend to successfully escape. Mason had kept me cooped up in his apartment, distracting me with cuddling and orgasms until I barely knew which way was up. And if I were honest, I didn't want to leave. I'd never felt so cared for, so tended to, so...safe. It was unbelievable that I got that from my stepbrother and bully, the same man who'd once terrorized me.

But the truth was right there. I saw it every time he brought me my favorite coffee (not drugged this time), made sure I came first, fed me my favorite foods, dropped kisses on my neck and forehead, held me in our sleep. I was becoming addicted to it, which terrified me. I hadn't changed my mind on where I stood. We couldn't be together. It would destroy our reputations—and our parents.

Also, I desperately needed a change of clothes. I'd been wearing his sweats every day because my one outfit was dirty, and I was sick of swimming in the fabric—even if I loved the comfort of having his smell surround me. Laundry was as good an excuse as any.

"You can do your laundry here," Mason argued. I was standing by the front door to the apartment, and he was leaning on the door, facing me and blocking my exit. I tried to ignore just how sexy he was, arms crossed over his chest, a slight smirk on his face, as he propped up the door.

"My clothes are at my dorm," I said. "What am I supposed to do, go get my clothes and bring them back here? That makes no sense."

"It makes complete sense. I'll come with you."

"Mason." Frustration filled me. I needed space so I could process everything that had happened between us. And he wasn't going to give it to me.

"I need to go practice at the studio, too," I pointed out.

"I'll come with you." He wasn't backing down. "I want to watch you dance, butterfly. I've never seen you dance."

His words melted me. "How about I go home, do laundry, do some work, and you meet me at the studio later?"

"Bro," Matt said from the living room. "You can't. We're supposed to meet the team at the gym in twenty."

Relief and disappointment battled it out in my heart. I loved the idea of him being with me, but I needed some time on my own. Mason having gym time with the team was perfect.

Mason groaned. "Fuck. Butterfly, come to the gym with us."

Oh, lord.

"Why?"

"Because I don't want you out of my sight for a second," he said. "Besides, you can be my counterweight."

As appealing as the image was of him doing push-ups with me on his back, I needed to stick to my plan. Space. Thinking. Clean clothes. Dance.

"And *I* don't want to show up at the gym wearing your

sweats that barely fit me, or my dirty clothes. It screams walk of shame."

He pushed off from the door and took two steps toward me, until he towered over me and I had to crane my neck back to look up at him. "No shame. Remember?"

"I remember," I said gently, even if my body didn't believe it.

He shook his head. "I'll come get you tonight."

I started to protest, but he lifted a hand to my cheek, cradling my face as he swallowed my mouth in a dizzying kiss. I moaned, surrendering to him, until Matt disappeared. So did my shame about the forbidden nature of our relationship. How could I hold onto fear of the future when Mason's heat, taste, touch kept me in the present, making me feel owned and cared for, all at once?

Finally, he released me. "I'll drop you off at your dorm."

I shook my head, needing at least a little independence. "I can walk."

He shook his head. "Butterfly, I don't think you understand yet. You're mine. That means when I say *I'll drive you*, I'm driving you. It's my job to keep you safe and comfortable."

"Fifteen minutes," Matt called in warning.

"C'mon, Butterfly. Do you want me to be late?"

I relented. "Fine, you can drive me."

A grin spread across Mason's face. "Good girl."

WHEN MASON DROPPED ME OFF, HE DRAGGED ME INTO another dizzying kiss before setting me free. Lost in the memory of his lips on mine and already missing him, I almost didn't see Chris skulking past me in the hallway.

"Oh!" I said, surprised.

He shot backwards, like I'd burned him.

"I'm sorry," I started, then looked more closely at him, freezing in shock.

He was a mess. Two black eyes, his nose out of joint like it had been broken, a split lip. His left arm was in a sling.

"You," he spat. "You need to stay away from me."

"What happened?" I didn't like the guy—he was a complete creep, after all. But that didn't mean I wasn't concerned.

"Your jackass stepbrother is what happened," he said. "He didn't like that we were getting close, and he let me know with his fists."

"What?" I could barely get the word out, my heart was hammering so hard. "He couldn't have, I've been with him all weekend."

"It didn't happen this weekend. It happened on Thursday. He was waiting for me in my room when I got back from partying. Beat the shit out of me, told me to stay away from you. Which I've been trying to do. You need to get away from me. I don't want that psycho coming after me again."

I didn't understand. Refused to understand. I knew by now that Mason was jealous and possessive, and he hadn't liked that Chris had flirted with me, but there was no way he could have known that Chris had drunkenly come onto me in my room the other night.

And he'd promised me he wouldn't hurt anyone for me. That would have been the time to tell me, *oh, by the way, I beat up your RA.*

Which meant he'd lied to me.

He'd *lied.*

"No," I said, shaking my head. "He would've told me."

Chris raised a split eyebrow, then rubbed at it like it hurt him. "You sure about that? Because my face says differently. He didn't like that we almost hooked up the other night."

"We didn't almost hook up the other night," I said automatically, my brain spinning as I tried to figure out how Mason could have known about that.

Chris shook his head. "You fucking tease. Get away from me before you get me killed."

With that, he left me in the hallway, staring after him.

Back in my room, I paced trying to figure out how Mason could have possibly known that Chris had harassed me in my room. Had someone overheard and told him? Had he been lurking outside? But if he had, why hadn't he stormed in here and come to my rescue?

And he'd *lied* to me. By omission, sure, but it was a lie just the same.

My father had lied to us, too.

A realization stopped me in my tracks. I immediately started scanning the small room for something unfamiliar, something out of place.

There.

I hadn't noticed it before, I was so distracted by how bad I'd needed to come, but the picture frame holding a photo of me, Bea, and my mom was out of place.

And in the corner was a small black dot.

With shaking hands, I lifted the frame and picked at the plastic and glass circle until it came free.

A camera.

And if there was one, that meant there were probably more.

Frantic and filled with an almost manic rage, I tore my room apart, searching books, other frames, my laptop, the wall, the bookshelf I'd built, the art on the walls. I wasn't sure how much time passed, but by the time I was done I was sweating and I'd found five other cameras.

Oh my god, he'd been watching me.

He'd been *watching me.*

For all I knew, he was watching me right now.

Maybe I could've forgiven the violence. I *hated* it, but I understood Mason well enough now. He'd been protecting me, and as horrible as it made me, it also made me feel safe. Besides, he'd done it before I'd shared my ultimatum with him.

But he'd *lied.* He could have told me what he'd done. That he'd beat up Chris, and that he'd placed cameras in my room. Even though, if I were honest, it was completely in line with who he was. Why wouldn't the man who'd drugged me so he could have sex with me set up cameras in my room so he could watch me without my knowledge or consent? He'd manipulated me, tortured me. How was lying to me any different? It all pointed to the same thing: he wanted me, but he didn't respect me. I was nothing more than a possession to him.

I couldn't trust him. Not now, not ever.

My phone began buzzing. Mason.

I must have missed a camera.

I picked up my phone to answer, then threw it on the bed. He'd have some excuse, some way to manipulate me back into his arms. No, I needed to be strong. I couldn't be with someone who bulldozed my desires for his own needs.

It kept buzzing, then finally fell silent.

It was almost a relief, having a reason to end things with him. This served as well as anything.

It's an excuse because you're scared.

Maybe. But I was clinging to it. He was, as Chris had said, psycho. He had no respect for my boundaries. If he'd gone this far to have me, how much further would he go? What else would he lie about? Would he one day grow bored of me, and turn to another woman? What if he already had? What if there was something going on with Emily, and I was the side piece, just like my mother had been?

I was spiraling. I knew it. But his actions had triggered my greatest fears, and I couldn't win against them. It was a good thing. If they were right, I'd get hurt. By my step-brother, of all people. This was still fucking wrong.

I was done. My heart hurt, and I climbed into bed, hiding under the covers. I was sure there was another camera, and I didn't want him to see me. I didn't want him to know how sad I was, or he'd use it against me.

I was so, so tired.

I'd end things tomorrow.

Of course, that's when the lock turned in my door and it opened, revealing an irate Mason.

22

LESLIE

"Of course you fucking have a key," I said.

He pushed into the room, closing the door behind him—and locking it.

"We can talk about that later. Right now, I want to know why you're ignoring my calls."

"Oh, fuck off," I said. "You know why."

"Fuck off?" His voice got low, quiet, dangerous. He advanced on me. "Last I checked, you were in this. And now you're telling me to fuck off? I'll tell you what we won't be doing. We won't be playing this game where you flip back and forth between admitting you want to be with me and hiding from me."

Even though there was some truth to what he was saying, it was only more manipulation. He thought it would work on me, that I'd give in. Lucky for him, I was about to disabuse him of that notion.

"Let me tell *you* what we won't be doing. We won't play like you care, like you respect me as a person, when you installed *these* in my bedroom and attacked my RA for getting drunk and stupid in my room. And *lied* to me about it." I held out one of the tiny cameras to him.

He stilled, giving me some satisfaction. At least he knew he'd fucked up.

"How'd you find the cameras?" he asked.

"It didn't take long to deduce, after I saw my RA's face," I said.

Mason's blue eyes turned to ice. "He confronted you? That asshole was supposed to leave you alone."

"No, I bumped into him in the hallway, and he told me what happened. Mason, it's one thing to be protective of me, it's another to use violence against someone who never hurt me. And it's a whole *other* thing to watch me without my permission. What I do in my room is private. It's *mine.*" I took a deep breath. "And that's not even the worst part—"

"And you're mine," he said, backing me against the bed. "I know you don't understand my tactics, but you belong to me. It's my job to keep you safe. If that means watching you, wherever you are, without your knowledge or consent, I'll do it. If it means hurting anyone who even thinks about touching you without your permission, I'll do it. If it means stepping in front of a bullet and dying to keep you safe, I'll do it. I fell down on the job before, because I wouldn't admit to myself that you belonged to me. I won't do it again."

His lips were an inch from mine. Less. He overwhelmed me with his heat, and the temptation to fall into his arms and let him do what he wanted. But I was stronger than that. I wasn't going to let him steamroll me. Not into a relationship, not into letting him do whatever he wanted, not into disappointing our parents.

"You lied," I reminded him.

"I didn't lie."

"Mason, we were in your bed, and I told you I never

wanted you to harm anyone for me. And instead of telling me, 'oops, I already did, it won't happen again,' you changed the subject! You've been invading my privacy for weeks, you drugged me to get me in bed. Those are all forms of lies. How the hell am I supposed to trust you?"

He spoke against my lips. "Trust that I'll keep you safe. Trust that I'll keep you close. Trust that I'll never let you go."

I shook my head, tears slipping from my eyes.

"I want you to leave."

"No."

I stood taller. He was so much bigger than me, but I wouldn't let him use his size to intimidate me.

"I don't think you understand," I said. "I am making a choice. I am using my agency. I am telling you: You aren't allowed to be here. I don't give you permission to be here. I don't give you permission to be with me. This, between us, whatever it was? It's done."

He reached forward, bracketing my throat with his big hand, squeezing lightly. Not hurting me, but the threat was there. "I don't think *you* understand," he said, his voice a menacing seduction of silk and velvet. "I'm not going anywhere. If I wanted to, I could have you on your back in your bed in moments, and be inside you moments later."

My heart raced with fear—and if I were honest, desire.

I stared at him levelly. "You could. You could make me do all sorts of things I don't want to do. But I would hate you for it."

"No, you wouldn't," he argued. "You want me, butterfly. You don't want me to leave, not really. You think you're not supposed to want me, not allowed to accept my version of care, so you're looking for any excuse to push me away. This is an excuse."

I pushed against his chest. "It's not, though. Mason,

you're scary. You scare me. I know who I am, and it's not someone who fucks her stepbrother. It's not someone who condones violence, and it's certainly not a doormat who lets her boyfriend walk all over her and lie to her."

He stared at me, a look in his eyes I couldn't read.

"And you really feel this way." He didn't bother to make it a question.

I swallowed. "Yes."

"And you'd really hate me if I didn't give you a choice."

"Yes."

The word was like a dagger in my throat. Because he was right. I wanted him. But I wanted to be someone I could look at in the mirror and like who I saw more.

He dropped his hands and stepped back.

"Then I guess this is goodbye."

"I guess it is."

He shook his head. "I expected more from you, butterfly. I don't want you to be a doormat, I want you strong. If you want to fight me, fight me. But you want to fly away..."

He muttered something under his breath as he walked the few steps to the door, and reached on top of it, plucking the last camera off the wall.

"Goodbye, Daddy," I whispered, swallowing back my tears.

Pain and anger tightened his jaw. "Lock the door behind me."

And then he was gone.

I collapsed on the bed and let myself cry.

23

LESLIE

"Come in," Professor Evans called.

I entered her office. It was bright and light and cluttered with more books than I'd ever seen in my life outside of a library. I loved it immediately.

The professor herself sat behind her desk, staring at her phone. If I didn't know better, I'd think she was blushing behind her glasses.

"Are you okay?" I asked her.

She looked up from her phone, smiling gently. "Of course. Just got caught up with this stupid little box of technology. Don't ever let anyone tell you that Millennials aren't as addicted to their phones as your generation is."

I laughed, a little weakly. I wasn't looking forward to this conversation.

"So how can I help you, Ms. Berger?"

"It's about the partnered project for class."

She sat back in her chair, eyes trained on mine. "What about it?"

"I'd like to see about changing partners. Or if I can even do it myself."

"Hmm." She took her glasses off and carefully folded them before placing them on the desk in front of her. "It's a little late to change partners. The outline for your presentation and paper are due tomorrow."

"So then let me do it alone," I practically begged.

"The point of this project is to get you all comfortable with partnered projects. Often, those come with...friction."

I tried not to blush at the word friction, and Professor Evans was kind enough to pretend not to notice that I failed.

"Do you want to talk about it?"

"Mason and I..." the words caught in my throat. I tried again. "We don't see eye to eye on a number of things."

"Hmm." She closed her eyes for a moment, and I waited, my feet tapping out their anxiety on the floor. I didn't know how much she knew—I'd die if she knew about the sex—but the subtext in her words made it clear she knew that there was more to my relationship with Mason than stepsiblings and project partners.

Opening them, she smiled again. "In any sort of project, compromise is hard, especially if the partners have different...end goals. *Especially* if one of the partners isn't sure what their end goal is."

"I—I don't know what to say."

She nodded. "You don't have to say anything, not to me at least. I recommend talking through the friction with your partner so you can agree on a joint goal."

"What if it's not our goals, but our approach that we can't agree on?"

At that, she smiled. "A lot of the time, people—men especially—always use a hammer, because they can't imagine anything isn't a nail."

"So what do I do?"

She rose, lifting her hand to emphasize our time was up. "Give him a tool that isn't a hammer."

OUTSIDE HER OFFICE, I TEXTED MASON.

can we talk?

The bubbles appeared, disappeared. Nothing.

we need to work on our project

our outline is due tomorrow

unless you want to fail a class your first semester of college...

Words appeared. I knew that would get him.

meet me at my place

I couldn't go back to his suite.

no, mine

you really want me in your space?

Good point.

the library then

no library

I got my ass handed to me at practice today and need a soft surface

I was annoyed at myself for how worried his words made me. I immediately wanted to comfort him, bring him ice, give him a massage—anything to help him feel better.

But hadn't he done the same for me?

fine

I'll meet you at your place in twenty

Bubbles appeared. Then:

have you eaten?

that's not anything for you to worry about

He saw right through me. Of course he did.

I'll make sure I have something for you when you get here

His words sent tingles through me, damn him. Even though they were so bossy.

Professor Evans' words echoed in my head. *Give him a tool that isn't a hammer.*

Was there a way for me to teach Mason that he didn't have to control me in order to have me, he just had to care about me?

And was it even worth it to try? Or would I just end up with a bruised—or worse—broken heart?

When I got to his suite, I hesitated outside the door. I

hadn't seen him since I'd ended things—was it really a good idea to be in his space with him again?

But he'd agreed with me, hadn't he? He'd left, and he hadn't said a word since.

"Door's open," he called. His voice sounded gruff.

I pushed it open. He lay on the couch, shirtless, eyes closed. As I slowly moved toward him, I gasped. Bruises peppered his ribs and abs, barely visible now, but they'd be black and blue tomorrow.

"Can you get me the ice out of the freezer?"

I grabbed it for him, and crossed to the couch. But instead of handing it to him, I carefully pressed it on his chest, feeling a need to help, to soothe his pain.

"What happened?"

He cracked open an eye. "Had some extra aggression to get out today. Things got a little heated during practice."

"Why'd they get heated?" I asked, moving the ice pack to another part of his chest as he sighed.

"Someone said something I didn't like. Had to make it clear they weren't going to say it again."

"What did they say?"

He opened his other eye but didn't say anything.

"Oh. You mean they said something about me."

He shrugged, then groaned. "They won't do it again, butterfly."

"We talked about this. You can't beat up anyone who says or does anything bad to me."

He raised a hand, brushing it down my cheek. "Watch me."

Feeling awkward at the touch, and the heat that spread through me, I moved away, leaving the ice pack to slide down his chest. "Where are your roommates?"

"Emory has a night class and Matt is at his boyfriend's. There's Thai food coming. I got you Pad See Ew."

My favorite. Once again he knew all my secrets; I wished I knew all of his.

But what could I say? Other than: "Thank you."

He waved this off. "I've realized that feeding you is one of my greater joys in life."

"Mason. You can't talk that way."

"Sorry," he said, but he didn't sound sorry. "We should get started on the outline. C'mon, come sit. I won't bite."

Sure, like I believed that. Still, I sat, leaving space between us and feeling disappointed when he didn't try to fill it with his body against mine. And angry at myself for feeling disappointed in the first place. We worked for a while, talking through the project, until the food came.

I got up to get it, serving it onto plates and bringing them to him on the couch. We ate silently, until:

"How are you?" he asked.

What was he even playing at?

"How do you think I am?" I asked him.

"I assume relieved, and feeling free, now that I'm out of your life. Or maybe I'm wrong, and you're regretful. Lonely, even."

I glared at him, started to get to my feet, ready to get the hell out of there. His hand shot out and gripped my wrist. It felt like a shackle, and what's worse was that I liked it.

"Stay, Leslie."

"Or what?" I asked, my heart speeding up.

"Or I'll make you stay."

"Yeah?" My heart beat even faster. I needed to go, but he'd done something to my brain, because his behavior triggered my desire now. Again with the Pavlovian response! "I don't believe you."

"Are you being a brat on purpose, butterfly? Because if so..." In one smooth move, he flipped me onto my stomach. "...if so, I'm going to have to punish you—again."

And before I could protest or pull away, he delivered three sharp slaps to the underside of my ass. These spanks made the last session feel like child's play. I tried to squirm away, but he planted one of his arms across my lower back, pinning me where I was.

Just like the butterfly he called me.

24

MASON

She was trapped, right where I wanted her.

Once again, I thought she'd come back to me. That giving her some space would mean she'd pursue me for once. I'd been patient, methodical, even asking Matt to smack me around a little to make myself look extra sympathetic.

And this time? I'd been right.

Oh, I knew she was still angry—and she had valid reasons to be. I shouldn't have kept the truth about what I'd done from her. But when she'd issued that ultimatum, I'd weighed the pros and cons of telling her I'd beaten her RA to a pulp for making her uncomfortable.

Pro: Honesty made for a healthier foundation in a relationship.

Con: She'd dump my ass, and then I *would* have to kidnap her to a deserted island. I doubted my dad would ignore a charge that large on my Amex.

Sometimes being eighteen was such bullshit. I'd been a prince all my life—it was time to become a king.

Leslie was also pissed about the cameras. I hadn't set

myself up as the most trustworthy guy, and I'd fix that going forward—but she also had to learn how to forgive me for doing fucked up things in the name of her happiness.

And *that* was the lesson I was about to teach her.

I delivered a series of slaps to her ass, ignoring her cries of outrage, growing hard at the sight of the pale skin of her upper thighs turning a deep pink.

She wiggled on my lap, and I grew even harder. I reached under her to unbutton her shorts—her fucking tiny shorts, as if she had a right to show off her legs to any fucking leech on campus, when the only person who should be seeing her legs was me. I slipped my hand into her underwear.

Wet, just like last time.

"This turns you on, doesn't it, baby? You like a little pain with your pleasure. Is that why you make Daddy so angry by sending him away? Because you need attention? Need him to prove he'll do anything to have you? Don't worry. Daddy will give his butterfly all the attention she needs, even if what she needs is a hard spanking."

I ripped her shorts and panties down to her ankles.

Shocked, she fought me. It was cute, that she thought she could take me on and win.

"Mason, stop it!"

That deserved an extra hard slap, which I delivered—right between her legs.

"That's not what you call me when your clothes are off, remember?"

She moaned but didn't give me what I needed.

"I won't stop until you apologize to your Daddy," I warned. "I don't care if your skin turns black and blue, and if you can't sit for a week. It's what you need, and what you deserve."

She moaned again, and I felt her grow wetter. I gathered the wetness in her little slit and used it to rub her clit, which began to harden and strain under my touch. She shook on top of me.

But she didn't give in.

I sighed. "Butterfly, I should've been honest with you. It was a mistake, and I won't keep secrets from you anymore. But that means you have to accept what I do."

"Do for who?" she gasped as I continued to play with her. "For you?"

"No, butterfly," I said, voice stern, delivering a small, stinging slap to her clit.

She shrieked, writhing on my lap. I held her tighter, so she had nowhere to go.

"Everything I do, I do for *you*. For *us*," I continued. "Do you hear me?"

"Yes, but no more lies, Mason."

I delivered another slap to her clit. "Who?"

"Daddy," she cried, like it was a relief to say again. "Please, Daddy."

"What are you asking Daddy for?"

It was so quiet I had to strain to hear her.

"Please, Daddy...more."

So I gave her what she wanted, alternating between rubbing her clit and spanking her ass. Her ankles were trapped by her shorts, and she had nowhere to go. I was beginning to learn that when Leslie felt trapped, it only turned her on more.

"My good little butterfly," I told her, thrusting a finger inside her tight little pussy. My cock thickened, right against where her clit was. Pausing for a moment, I pulled my own shorts down, freeing my cock so it rubbed directly against her cunt, skin to skin. I almost shot off, then and there.

"Do you feel Daddy's cock? He's so big and hard for you," I growled. "He feels you getting wet and ready to take him. Right where he belongs."

I thrust two fingers inside her this time. She was still tight but her wetness eased the passage and her arousal loosened her inner muscles enough to ease my way. She was sopping wet, dripping all over my leg and cock. All for me.

It reminded me of what I had to do today. I gritted my teeth, tempted to call it off. It was going to kill me, but it was for *her*, and I'd do anything for her.

Well, this I'd only do once.

"Please, please, please," she begged me, solidifying my decision. She needed me—to make her come, and to give her the things she couldn't even articulate to herself. I felt her wriggle, like if she shifted enough my cock would pop right inside of her.

I was going to play with her first.

"Oh no you don't," I ordered. "You don't come and you don't get Daddy's cock until you tell me what I want to hear."

She hiccupped. I lifted her up so I could see her face. Tears of need, desire, and shame covered her face.

"I'm—sorry, Daddy."

Finally.

I gentled my voice. "What are you sorry for, baby?"

"I don't know," she wailed. "But being away from you makes me feel terrible, even though I know it's the right thing to do. I'm sorry for kicking you out. I'm sorry for wanting you so badly I can't think straight. I hate this."

Something in me snapped, and all the emotion I'd been withholding from her came pouring out.

"You need to stop running away from this, from us," I said, throat tight. "Say sorry for pushing Daddy away, and letting fear of what other people will say get in the way of what we both need—each other. Stop letting what you think you *should* feel get in the way of what you do feel."

"I'm scared," she admitted, wiping her eyes. "I'm scared you're changing me, and that no one will accept us. I don't know what to do with that feeling." I rewarded her for her honesty by peppering her face with kisses, tracking where her tears had fallen. I wrapped my arms around her and rocked her.

"It's okay, baby. You're here now. I think you need a distraction. Get on your knees."

I expected her to hesitate, but she looked at me, bright eyed, and kneeled in front of me.

I didn't have to prompt her this time, she took my cock in her hand and lowered her mouth over me, sucking hard.

I gathered her hair in my hand, tugging. She moaned around me.

"My butterfly is a quick learner, isn't she? You're sucking me so well, sweetheart. Daddy needs to go deeper. Breathe through your nose," I coached her, and slowly sank deeper into her mouth until I touched the back of her throat. My cock was too long for her mouth, so I used her hair like reins and tilted her head until her throat opened and my cock slid inside. Her eyes widened in panic.

"You're okay. You can take me, butterfly. You want to be Daddy's little slut, don't you? This is how." I raised my hips, thrusting deeper, until she'd swallowed me all the way to the base of my cock. I held her there for a few moments, and she swallowed around my cock.

I needed to come, but I wasn't wasting my seed on her throat. No, I was saving all of it for her pussy. And maybe her little ass later, if we got that far.

I withdrew from her mouth, smiling at Leslie's sweet whining. She didn't want to give me up.

I tugged her to her feet. "On the couch, face down, ass up, butterfly."

Just then, the door opened, and Emory entered the suite.

Just like I'd planned.

This was going to hurt so fucking much. I was going to hate every fucking second of it.

But I remembered that first night together, when a blissed out Leslie had told me her deepest, darkest fantasy.

Yes, this would kill me.

But if it gave her what she wanted, it would be worth it.

25

MASON

Emory had frozen when he saw us—his eyes scanning Leslie's body, eyes growing hooded. He wanted her. I wanted to kill him for it, even though this was exactly what I'd planned. And I'll confess—I was a little turned on by it. He couldn't have her, only I could, but he could play with her—once.

Leslie's breathing had quickened. She started to cover her pussy with her hands, but I stopped her, pulling them behind her back and gripping them. She cowered against me, but she was even more turned on—I could smell it.

There it was: proof.

"Dude, your room is right there." Emory motioned behind him.

"Remember when we were kids and the teacher would tell us it wasn't fair to bring a snack unless there was enough to share with the class?"

"I remember." There was a glint in Emory's eyes. "You saying what I think you're saying?"

"No," Leslie tried to deny us—and herself.

"You want this," I told her. "You told me as much, butterfly. Consider it a gift to you—and an apology." To Emory I said, "You can't fuck her pussy or ass, but everything else is fair game."

I kissed Leslie's hair.

"You want a distraction? You want to feel better? This is it."

"But I don't want him," she objected. But the wetness glistening on her thighs told a different story.

I swatted her ass. "Honesty goes both ways, butterfly."

She gasped. "How—"

"You told me the night I took your pussy for the first time. And I'll give you anything—everything you want."

"But—" she protested, but it was half-hearted.

I changed tactics. "You want me, don't you? And you want to please me?"

She nodded.

"Good."

I moved to the couch, lifting her up and then placing her right above my lap. She was still tight—she'd only lost her virginity to me a week ago—so it took some leverage but I finally got her to slide down my cock until she was wrapped around all of it. So tight and hot, and she'd just had her mouth around me, and I needed to come.

Not yet, I ordered myself. This was for her.

Emory swaggered toward us, unzipping his jeans and pulling out his cock. Where I was long and curved, Emory was short, but thick. Leslie was going to have a hard time getting her mouth around him.

Good.

He stood above her, his cock in line with her face. He looked at me.

"I want to touch her tits," he said.

"Butterfly, take your top off," I told her. She hesitated, and I smacked her hip. In response, she clenched around me.

Fuck.

I focused on holding in my come, even though my balls ached.

"Now," I said.

Slowly, her hands trembling, she pulled her tank top over her head, revealing her small, perky breasts. I bent my head so my chin rested on her shoulder. I didn't want to miss the show.

Emory started stroking her tits, circling her nipples until they were tight to what must have been the point of pain. Then he began pinching them.

"Suck on his balls," I ordered her. "Put your whole mouth around them. That's it. Good girl."

Emory exhaled, distracted from playing with her tits. His cock hardened, slapping her face.

I took over for him. Pinching her nipples in a continuous rhythm. Her pussy started clenching to the same beat. I was playing her like a fiddle, and I fucking loved it.

Emory pulled his balls from her mouth. "She's gotta open wider, or I'll never fit," he said.

"Daddy needs you to open wide for his friend," I said.

"I'm trying," she whined.

"I'll help." Using my free hand, I hooked my fingers in her cheek, pulling until her jaw widened. Emory raised an eyebrow. I'd never touched his cock before, but there was a first time for everything.

He shoved his cock in her mouth, the side touching my knuckles. It was an interesting sensation, but it was the way

Leslie's cheeks bulged and her pussy started clenching around me that really turned me on.

"Ah, fuck," Emory said. "Watch your teeth."

I growled. "Careful how you talk to her."

He shook his head. "*Please* watch your teeth, Leslie."

"Better." Satisfied, I went back to pinching her tits, throwing in a slap every once in a while to keep things interesting. Emory matched my rhythm, thrusting in her mouth.

Terrified, Leslie reached out a hand, searching for one of mine. I linked our fingers together and squeezed. She calmed, surrendering once again.

Mine. I fought off the part of me who wanted to strangle him for getting near her, much less having his cock in her mouth. But it was my hand she was holding. He was an interloper, that was all.

"How deep can I—" Emory began.

Protectiveness rose in my chest. "Don't choke her and go slow. She's my good girl but she's new to this."

Leslie moaned around his cock in agreement.

He slowly began thrusting in and out of her mouth, grunting. I moved the hand not holding hers from her tits down her stomach, feeling her tremble from my touch.

"Poor butterfly," I murmured in her ear. "Getting it from both ends from your former bullies. You must be so overwhelmed. You must need to come so badly, you probably hate that, don't you? No coming until I say so."

She shuddered, but didn't orgasm. I was impressed by how well she was taking to my orders, but then she'd been made for me. Meant to be mine, so why wouldn't her body know its master? I began to rub her clit lightly, as Emory thrust deeper. She gurgled around his cock, clenching so tight around my cock, my balls felt like they were boulders.

It wouldn't take much, for either of us.

"Feel free to let loose now," I told Emory, who grunted in reply and picked up speed. It was quiet in the room, the only sounds the wet gurgles of Leslie's mouth and short gasps as she took in air, Emory's grunts, and my heavy breathing.

I sped up my circles and clit spanking. Leslie jerked in my arms, her body going stiff as a board.

There we go.

"A virgin a week ago, and you're already being spitroasted. You're Daddy's little slut now. You'll do whatever I tell you, butterfly? You love being controlled like this. It doesn't matter that he's in your throat, you're mine and mine alone." With that, I pinched her clit, and Leslie cried out again, her body jerking, cut off by Emory's cock.

"Fuck, I'm gonna," Emory choked.

"Not in her mouth," I ordered, and with a pained groan, he pulled out, jerked his cock once, twice, and came all over Leslie's tits. The degradation was pushing Leslie to her limits—and I still hadn't released her poor clit, which was pulsing between my thumb and forefinger.

Emory stumbled backwards, landing in an armchair facing the couch.

"Fuck, fuck, fuck," he chanted.

Time to make my fiddle play her tune. My cock was thick and desperate, and it deserved its reward for waiting for so long. And Leslie still hadn't come.

"Gonna fill you up with my come, little butterfly," I taunted, releasing her clit from its cage. "Train you to take my come now, so you're ready when I start breeding you later."

That did it. She shrieked, loud enough to bring down the walls as she pulsed around me, her walls squeezing my cock. I didn't even need to thrust, the pressure enough to light my balls on fire as I came, unleashing a tide of neverending come, filling her up to the brim. It was like my cock had never come before, because I kept coming, feeling it drip down her pussy and back onto my balls, which made me spurt all over again.

Emory watched.

"You lucky fucking asshole," he said once I'd finished. Leslie trembled against me, breathing heavily, aftershocks making her clench around me in small jerks. I rubbed her stomach gently, calming her.

"That was a one and done," I told him. "Consider it a gesture of goodwill for keeping this between us for so long."

"Yeah, sure," he muttered, standing, rezipping his jeans, and leaving the room.

"That was, that was," Leslie was gasping.

"That was a one time thing for you, too," I told her. "I figured it was only fair for you to get to have one other cock —but that's the last one. You fantasized about this, and I promised to fulfill your fantasies. *Once.* For the rest of our lives, the only cock you'll ever have in your mouth is mine, the only hands you'll have on your perfect little tits are mine. Got it?" Under my breath, I added. "You have no idea how much that killed me."

"Then why'd you do it?" she murmured.

"Because I have one purpose in life, and that's making you happy. Do you get it now, butterfly?"

She blinked, understanding coming to her eyes. "Yes."

I jostled her. "Yes, what?"

"Yes, Daddy."

"Good girl. I stood up, lifting her into my arms. "I'll get you cleaned up and then we should work on this assignment, shouldn't we?"

"I don't think my brain is working," she told me.

I laughed and kissed her. "I'll do most of the work. I've been doing most of it so far, anyway."

"Hey," she slapped me. She was so much easier with me after she orgasmed. I needed to remember that. I didn't know how long it would last this time, before she remembered the stepsiblings of it all.

"Don't worry, butterfly. I'll always do the work for you."

26

LESLIE

Mason carried my limp body into the bathroom, locking the door.

"*Now* you care about someone seeing me naked?" I asked.

I couldn't believe him—or what had just happened. I'd fantasized about being fucked by two guys at once since I'd stumbled across it in a romance novel, but I'd never thought it would come true. The fantasy shamed me, even as I got myself off to it.

And Mason had asked, listened, and delivered. Even though he'd hated it.

I have one purpose in life, and that's making you happy.

At that moment, my heart—which had already wandered to the edge—tripped and fell off the cliff, falling down, down, down.

I was in love with my stepbrother.

I was going to hell.

Unaware of my thoughts, Mason set me on the sink and tilted my chin to look up at him. "Do you think I was kidding when I said that was your only time with someone else—ever? I wanted to show you that there's nothing to be ashamed of. Not what you crave, and not being with me. You're beautiful, and desirable, and Emory has no issues with us together—he thinks it's hot. People will be okay with us in time, butterfly, I promise."

I started to protest, but he put a finger to my lips. "Just think about it, okay? There's nothing to worry about. I'll take care of you."

With that, he started the shower, fiddling with the knobs and testing it on his inner wrist like I deserved the care a baby did. Once he was satisfied with the temperature, he returned to me, lifting me back up and carrying me into the shower. He slowly and gently washed me, paying special attention to where Emory had come on my breasts.

"Gotta get him off you," he muttered.

I was exhausted. My body was wrung out with pleasure, my brain was burned out on confusion and uncertainty. I didn't want to have to make big decisions, or fight him, or argue with him, or argue with myself. I didn't want to do a school project, or try to act normal—whatever the hell that meant. What I wanted was to collapse in bed and sleep for a year. And I wanted Mason's big body wrapped around mine, protecting me from everything and blocking out the world, when I did.

I loved him. The joy in it scared me shitless.

"If you're so annoyed about it, why did you let him in the first place?" I asked.

Mason paused. "Besides you wanting it? I need you to realize how desirable you are. I know that all the bullying I did this summer did a number on you, but you need to know, butterfly..." his throat worked. "...There's nothing more desirable in the world than you. You're perfect to me, and nothing you do will ever change that. I need you. I've always needed you, since I first laid eyes on you. I love you, Leslie."

My heart stuttered at his words, and then it was like it leapt out of my chest and hovered between us, uncertain of where to go next.

It was one thing for me to love him, unrequited. In a way, that was safer. The certainty of heartbreak was almost preferable to the uncertainty of our future. What if I finally got everything I'd never known I wanted, only to have to give it up?

Mason loved me?

He couldn't love me.

Was this what love was, for him? Possession, obsession, the need for control, dominance, and an unwavering determination to do whatever he needed to have me? If that's what love was, it scared me.

But maybe for Mason, love also meant care. Learning to make my favorite foods, even though he'd never cooked a day in his life. Carrying me around so I was safe in his arms. Giving me experiences I'd been afraid to want. Protecting me from harm. It wasn't a safe version of love, but maybe it was love, all the same.

"No response?" he asked lightly, but his eyes told a different story. I'd never seen him look vulnerable before. And just like that, my heart fell directly into his hands.

"I don't forgive you for what you did," I told him.

"I know," he said. "And like I told you—I'm not sorry for keeping you safe. But I am sorry for making you feel like your feelings don't matter. Nothing matters more."

"I'm scared," I admitted.

"Then trust me," he said, tilting my chin up so I was forced to look directly in his eyes. "I promise I will do everything in my power to destroy anything and everything that scares you, butterfly."

I laughed. "Even if I don't want you to?"

"Even then. It's us, Leslie. Forever."

And even though I was still angry at him, I wanted to believe him—believe in him.

Could I?

27

LESLIE

"You stood me up last week. Did you forget about tequila-oh-clock?" Lucy stood outside my dorm room, arms crossed, chin jutted out.

Tequila. That's what I needed.

"Got stuck doing an assignment," I told her.

"Hmm." She surveyed me as I unlocked my door, following me in.

I collapsed on my bed and she hopped up and joined me.

"You don't look like you were doing an assignment. You look like you just climbed a mountain and barely lived to tell the tale."

I sighed, putting my head in my hands.

"Here. Have some medicine and tell Auntie Lucy all about it."

I took the bottle out of her hand, uncapped it, and tipped it into my mouth.

"It burns so good," I said, wiping my mouth and handing it back.

"Whoa, girl. Save some for the fishes." She shook her

head but chugged back some tequila herself. "Damn. Next time, remind me to bring limes."

I laughed.

She handed the bottle back. "Talk to me. This is about the hockey god, right?"

I groaned. "It is, but I don't want to talk about it."

She gaped at me. "Do you not have any girlfriends? This is how you bond, by sharing secret, outlandish stories about the guys you're fucking and commiserating in generalities about how evil men are, but how much we still like their dicks."

She was right. But if it got out that I had fucked my stepbrother...

"How about this? I'll tell *you* about the much-too-old-for-me man I've had my eye on, and the trouble I've gotten into with him, and you keep drinking. And once you're drunk and realize that I've given you the weapon to destroy me with, you can share, too. It'll be mutually assured destruction," she said happily.

"I'm going to need a lot more of this," I said, taking another huge swig of the tequila and passing it back to her.

"Okay, so, it goes like this. You know the head hockey coach?"

I nodded. I'd seen Mason's coach all over Tabb's Instagram. He was an attractive man, probably in his late thirties, and had been hired this year. He seemed stern and like he would put up with zero bullshit. He was also the son of the CEO of a multibillion dollar corporation, and I wondered why he was working here, or working, at all.

"Well." Lucy lowered her voice. "He's my guardian."

I stared at her. "Like, as in, your dad?"

She reared back. "No, ew. My dad was his mentor, and

when he and my mom died, they left me to him in their will."

"Oh, Lucy, I'm so sorry," I said, placing a hand on her shoulder.

She gave me a small, pained smile in thanks. "Anyway, I was fifteen when he became my guardian, and I barely see him. The times we do, he treats me like a little girl. But now I'm finally nineteen years old, and I decided to make my move."

My jaw dropped. Literally. "You mean..."

"Uh huh." She blushed but lifted her head. "It's gonna happen. And I may end up needing your help."

As I digested this information, she took another swig of the tequila, then looked at the bottle. There were only a few fingers left.

"Shit, we've had a lot of this." She looked at me doubtfully. "Tomorrow's going to suck, isn't it?"

"It is." I stared back at her, and then we collapsed in a pile of giggles.

"Okay, your turn," she told me, when we came up for air. "It's only fair."

"Fine. It's like this. Mason—the hottie—is my..."

"Is your what?"

"My stepbrother." It came out on a croak.

She reared back. "Holy shit."

I nodded, feeling a little like a bobble head doll. "Exactly. Holy shit."

"And you two..."

"Yeah."

"For how long?"

"Just this past month."

"Did you grow up together?"

"No, our parents got married this summer. He hated me, or at least I thought he did. Made my life a living hell."

"But he doesn't hate you."

I shook my head. "He told me loves me. But how do I trust him, when he's done so many untrustworthy things? This could ruin my reputation—my *life.* And then what, he fucks around on me with someone else? Or worse, I become his dirty little secret?"

Just like my mom was.

Lucy giggled, shaking her head like I was a fool. "Girl."

"I mean it!"

Clearing her throat, she widened her eyes at me. "Leslie, that man does not look at you like you're a dirty little secret. I saw him staring at you in the cafeteria while he tried to make you jealous with that girl, and it was obvious to *everyone* that he wanted to eat you alive, for breakfast, lunch, *and* dinner. And then have you again for dessert." She shivered. "So fucking hot. And the way he slammed out of here, twice? If he wasn't serious, he wouldn't care that much. That man wants to lock you down and make *you* swallow the key."

She had no idea how right she was about that. I slumped, slightly relieved but still torn in two. "But he's my stepbrother. That's—"

"A little *Flowers in the Attic?*" I glanced at her. "What? I found it on my mom's bookshelf. And you've seen the movie, right? I mean, I don't think it's as bad as you think it is. First," she started counting reasons off on her fingers. "You two aren't *actually* related. Second, you didn't meet until you were practically adults, and you didn't start fucking until you were adults-adults. Third, they did it in *Clueless*, and it seemed fine."

Hope started to stir in me. I'd expected her to recoil from me, to march out of my room in disgust and tell everyone.

"You really think so?"

"Yes. That said, I'm in love with my guardian, so maybe I'm not the best judge here of what's kosher and what's not. Do your parents know?"

I shook my head, stress picking up in my chest at the thought. "No. No way. They'd never forgive either of us for that. And it might ruin their marriage—I couldn't do that to my mom. She's finally happy."

Lucy's eyes were wise and wide in her freckled face. "It's good that you care so much about your mom, but Leslie, have you ever thought about your own happiness? If other people's opinions didn't matter, if your mom and his dad gave you their blessing, what would you do?"

I looked down at my hands. "I'd be with him," I whispered. "I think...no, I *know* I love him."

"Wow. Okay then." She blinked, clearing her throat. "Do you want to look back at your life one year, five years, fifty years from now knowing you could have been with someone who made you happy, but you weren't because you were scared of what other people would think? What if he ends up with someone else? Would you ever be able to get over the fact that you gave up what you needed because you thought you *should*?"

"No. But you don't know what he did."

"What did he do?"

"Put cameras in my room, and then beat the hell out of Chris. And then he *lied* to me about it."

Her eyes got even bigger.

"Okay, the first one is fucked up, I won't deny it. But Chris is a creep, and probably deserved it. Did he deserve it?"

I sighed. "Yes."

"Look, some guys think we can't handle their truth. And if that's a dealbreaker for you, that's completely valid. But if it isn't...it's just another 'should' getting in the way of doing what's right for you. Is the violence or the secrecy a deal-breaker, or another hurdle? Because I won't lie, I think it's kind of hot. Toxic as fuck, but hot."

"A hurdle," I admitted.

"Well. Then." She dusted off her hands, temporarily forgetting the bottle of tequila was in one of them. It fell to the floor and rolled around. Fortunately, there was so little tequila left, no liquid spilled out.

"We should get that."

I hopped off the bed, but the room spun around me, and I fell on my knees. Giggling, I crawled over to the bottle.

"What are you doing down there?" Lucy asked.

"Retrieving the rest of our liquor," I told her. "Oh god, it's really gross down here on this carpet. Did they not like, clean it before we moved in?"

We both burst into another round of giggles...

...And the door burst open.

Mason framed the doorway, his golden hair in his eyes. Seeing him made me dizzy again—in an entirely different way. He scanned the room, landing on me.

"Leslie, what are you doing on the floor?" he asked.

"Swimming," I told him, and my silliness sent Lucy off into another round of giggles.

"You're drunk," he stated.

"Very," I chirped.

He glanced at Lucy. "You did this to her?"

She nodded.

"Nice work."

I peered up at him. "Are you being sarcastic, or serious? I

can't tell right now, my brain is too foggy to pick out your voice."

"Both."

"You aren't supposed to be here," I reminded him. "You were going out with the team tonight."

"I know," he said.

"And how'd you know I was drunk, anyway? Are there cameras I didn't find?"

He shook his head. "No. I missed you, so I ditched the guys to come here."

Oh.

My heart—well, I guess it was his now—melted even more.

Still. "You're interrupting girl bonding time," I told him.

"Nah," Lucy disagreed. "Getting laid is more important than us metaphorically braiding each other's hair. Besides, I'm too drunk to do a braid."

I flipped over, pointing at Lucy in accusation, the room spinning around me. "Betrayal!"

She giggled. "Thank me later," she singsonged.

And then I was being lifted into the air.

"If you puke on me, I'll take it out on your little ass, later," he said.

"Sounds fun," I informed him. "And I might. I've never had so much tequila in my life."

"Fucking awesome. Are you staying?" he asked Lucy.

"I don't want to deal with my roommates. Leslie, okay if I crash here?"

"My tiny bed is your tiny bed," I said.

"I hope not," Mason muttered, carrying me out the door and down to his car.

He had to pull over twice, because I puked twice. He held my hair back and rubbed my back.

He did that a lot that night. We spent more time in the bathroom together—this time wearing clothes. The room span, and my head swam, and the only constant, solid thing was Mason. I held tight to him like a life raft as the alcohol swept me somewhere terrible. I must've puked on him at least once, but unlike his threat, he never complained or scolded me, just got me into the shower, washed my hair, brushed my teeth for me, and helped me into his bed.

He disappeared briefly, then reappeared with a trash can, a bottle of coconut water, and some Advil.

"This should help," he told me, uncapping the bottle and holding it to my mouth as he handed me the pills. I obediently took a sip, swallowed the pills, and chugged the sweet, fresh-tasting drink. Then I collapsed onto the bed and he got in with me, pulling the covers up over both of us.

"I'm sorry I'm such a mess," I told him.

"I'm sorry I overwhelmed you so much you drank almost half a bottle of tequila," he told me.

"It was a small bottle."

"Still."

"I'm still worried. I don't know how this is going to work. But, Mason..."

"I know, butterfly. Shh. Go to sleep. We'll talk about it in the morning."

28

LESLIE

My head hurt. My mouth hurt. My whole fucking body hurt.

I rolled over, bumping straight into a warm, naked body.

Mason. He mumbled in his sleep, nuzzling into my neck.

The night before came rushing back to me, and I groaned. Why had I drunk so much, and why had I told Lucy everything?

Because you need a friend.

"I'm never drinking again," I muttered.

Mason laughed behind me. His voice was raspy-warm with sleep. "Everyone says that when they're hungover. They never actually stick with it."

"Did we..."

He snorted.

"Fuck? No. You puked on me three times. Kind of a mood killer."

But he didn't deny he might have been in the mood otherwise, even though I was drunk and my decision-making skills were impaired. Of course he didn't care; the first time we'd had sex, he'd drugged me, after all.

Still. He'd taken care of me through the night, and I didn't know a lot of guys who would take care of a woman and still hold her in the morning after she'd puked all over them multiple times.

"My hero," I said.

He kissed the back of my neck, sending shivers along my spine. "I hope so."

He got out of bed, walking around to my side. I admired his bare ass, tight and muscular, as he bent over and pulled on a pair of sweat shorts.

As he went to the door, I asked, "Where are you going?"

"To get you more coconut water. You're probably dehydrated and need the electrolytes."

"Why not Gatorade?"

He shuddered. "Because it tastes disgusting."

"Wait, does...does Emory know I'm here?"

He narrowed his eyes at me. "Why? Do you want to see him?"

Wait, was he...?

"Oh my god, you're jealous," I cried.

He shook his head. "There's no reason to be jealous. Guys are only jealous when they think there's a possibility they could lose their girl to another guy. I know I'm not going to lose you to him. That said, you don't get to be excited to see him. Remember: it was a one time thing."

"I'm not excited to see him, idiot. I'm embarrassed."

"Oh." He visibly relaxed. "There's no reason to be. He knows better than to mention anything about it; if he makes you uncomfortable, I'll cut off his balls. If anyone ever makes you uncomfortable, butterfly, I'll make them regret it.

And before you get all pacifist on me, that's not up for negotiation. I'll always tell you the truth, but you have to—"

"—Accept you. I know," I said.

His words warmed me. I never thought that Mason could be sweet—I'd only ever seen him as my evil tormentor. So it meant a lot that he cared so much about my feelings.

"What if it's a woman?"

He shrugged. "Like Emily? I'll think of something."

At Emily's name, I felt something in me go tight and painful.

"Why would you offer to hurt a woman you liked?" I asked.

He stared at me for a bit, like he was trying to figure something out. Then he smiled.

"You're right, I do like Emily."

"Great." I clenched my jaw against the tears that threatened to fall. Of course he liked her.

"I like Emily just fine," he continued. "Don't care if she's around, certainly not going to save her from a burning building. I like her, butterfly, but I love *you*."

"Oh." My heart started racing. He'd said that before. "But if you loved me, you wouldn't have lied to me. You wouldn't have drugged me. You wouldn't—"

He cut me off. "You're thinking of sitcom love, romcom love. Antiseptic, perfect, not messy at all. Boring. That's not real love, butterfly. When I say I love you, I mean the messy, dirty, dark, obsessive, can't think about anything or anyone else, don't care about anything else, kind. I'm *in* love with you, butterfly. That means I'll do anything to make you happy, and safe, and mine. That might mean something else for another man, but the only man you're getting is me, so the only kind of love you're getting is mine."

I couldn't admit it out loud, but his was the only kind of love I wanted.

29

MASON

It took everything I had, but when Leslie was feeling better, I let her leave on her own. I didn't pretend to let her go, only to follow her back to her dorm and break in while she was sleeping—although I considered it. I didn't have cameras in her room anymore (I hadn't been lying), so I had no idea what she was doing. But she'd softened toward me so much while she'd been hungover, I didn't want to destroy the new softness by forcing or sneaking my way in.

Emory and Matt had approved.

"She needs to know she's free to make her own choices, bro," Emory had said.

She wasn't. If I didn't think that I was *this* close to her admitting she loved me, if I wasn't positive that she was going to choose me, I would never have let her leave.

And.

If I were honest with myself, I wanted, no, *needed* that from her. I needed her to choose me. I'd keep her even if she didn't, but my stupid heart, the masochistic fucking thing, wanted her to tell me she loved me, to decide to be with me, despite the way it would affect her reputation or fuck with her idea of right and wrong.

So I'd let her leave with a kiss on her forehead and a promise to come to hockey practice later that day.

Now it was later, and I was regretting my words. We were in the middle of a scrimmage, first string against second string. And we were kicking ass. The puck was mine, and I was skating toward the other team's net, 90% of my focus on scoring, 10% on Leslie's absence. This was my moment to prove myself—to the team, to Coach. I wanted her here to witness it.

So far, she was nowhere to be seen.

Where was she?

"Head in the game, Calloway!" Coach called.

Fuck.

He was right.

The first string goalie was watching, eyes on the puck, on me. If I was a more basic player, I'd try to fool him with a single deke, or some amateur head fake. But I wasn't some basic player, and I was going to perform as if Leslie was in the stadium.

Approaching the net at a slower speed, I faked a shot to the left. The goalie raised a glove to intercept it, but I'd already pulled the puck back across my body before flicking it into the net. It sailed right past him.

The Datsyuk Deke. It was my favorite move, and it had worked.

There was cheering from the stands.

"Fuck yeah!" I said, proud, but my heart wasn't in it, because as I scanned the rink, I didn't see Leslie anywhere.

Dejected and angry, I lined up and congratulated the first string on the team. The center pulled me in. "Play like that, and I'm going to have to watch out for my spot," he said, before clapping me on the back.

"Thanks, man," I said.

A woman whistled. I looked up, and there was...Emily, walking down the stairs toward the ice, wearing a jersey with my number, 42, on it.

It was how old my mom was when she'd died.

"Mason?"

Emily pouted, I guess sexily, her hands running through her red hair.

Jesus, this was the last thing I wanted to deal with. What I really wanted to do was call Emily out for being a bitch to Leslie and warning her off me, but I knew if I said anything, it would drive her toward vengeance. And I knew Leslie would be pissed if I hit the redhead with my car or something, no matter how much of a bitch she'd been.

"Emily," I said easily, pulling my helmet off.

She smiled, relieved. She hadn't known how I'd react, after all. "I haven't seen you in a while." She approached me and attempted to touch my sweaty face, but I grabbed her wrist. Not painfully—I wasn't a dick—but hard enough to make my disapproval clear.

"Emily, no."

"What? Why?" she blushed, embarrassed.

"Emily, we've never fucked. I don't know why you act like you have some claim to me."

Her soft blush turned to an angry maroon. "I *thought* you liked me. You did, until *she* got in your head and fucked around in there. Seriously, Mace, what do you see in her?"

I shook my head. "Don't call me Mace. And don't *ever* touch me again. I mean it, Emily. You won't like what happens."

Only one person got to call me that from now on.

A person who was making her way down the stands, her own cheeks a pretty pink.

I dropped Emily's wrist, standing up straight but not defending myself. This would be a test. Would Leslie trust me? Would she believe I hadn't been hitting on Emily? Would she defend her territory—me—or would she run away again?

Be brave, butterfly, I thought.

Lucy stood at Leslie's side, her eyes narrowed on Emily. I was glad to see that Leslie had a real friend. She deserved all the friends. She deserved the whole world, and I would give it to her—she just had to ask.

And to trust me.

C'mon, butterfly.

"Emily," she said calmly. "I know we're never going to be friends, but I'm happy to try to get along if you are. But that means you need to stop harassing my...harassing Mason."

Emily turned bright red.

I, on the other hand, was disappointed. Had Leslie been about to call me her boyfriend? Or admit publicly I was her stepbrother, even though it was pretty clear to everyone on campus we were so much more? I'd take either, but I wouldn't accept this shying away from the truth of us.

I caught Leslie's gaze. Held out my hand. She stared at it.

And as she considered, Emily made the decision for us. For her.

"Who are you calling a harasser, *brotherfucker*?" she said, the word echoing through the stadium.

30

LESLIE

B*rotherfucker.*

Brotherfucker.

That's what I was. A brotherfucker.

I couldn't catch my breath. The entire stadium—team, spectators, even the coach—had gone silent. The word—four syllables—echoed through the cavernous, cold space, unimpeded by whispers. I imagined it echoing throughout campus, so loud our parents could hear it all the way in Westchester.

Part of me wanted to run, to hide. To laugh, hysterically, because we'd been caught. No, I'd been caught. My worst sins now made public to the entire freshman class at Tabb.

Mason watched me. Concerned.

You okay? he mouthed.

You okay. You. Not him. Not embarrassed. Not worried about himself or his own reputation. Only concerned about me.

I shook my head, because I wasn't.

He turned his vitriol on Emily. "Don't you dare fucking talk to her that way."

"You both make me *sick*," she hissed back. "You're fucked in the head, you know. Could've had anyone. Could've had me. And you choose your sister?"

"Emily, I don't think you realize just how lucky you are that you're a woman, because if you weren't you'd be on the ground in pieces right now for hurting Leslie. If I were you, I wouldn't test it."

"No."

The word left my mouth before I realized it. I moved closer to where they stood, Mason on the ice, Emily on the edge of the boards. I reached her, staring her down. She was taller than me, by a bit, but she wasn't stronger than me. Wasn't braver than me. Wasn't *better* than me.

"I've got this," I told him.

A small smile slid across his sweat-covered face. "Of course you do, butterfly."

"Emily, don't you get tired?" I asked her. "Doesn't the envy and bitterness and pettiness ever just...exhaust you? It exhausts me, and I don't even live it—I'm just the person you decided to be envious of. I'm sorry Mason doesn't want you. I'm sorry you don't get to have everything you want in life, and the only way you've ever learned to cope with not getting what you want is by making other people your target. But Emily, if you spent even *half* of the energy you spend hating me for the fact that I have someone you want, on looking in the mirror and figuring out *why* that is...well, don't you think that might be a little more productive?"

Laughter around us. I whipped my head, catching the other players chuckling. "Don't laugh," I told the crowd. "Reveling in her embarrassment makes you no better than she is."

The room went quiet again. Except for a hum of approval from Mason.

I wasn't done. "I know you want him. I know it kills you that I'm with him. But did you ever think that, I don't know, maybe you aren't right for him? And maybe he and I are right for each other? Yes, he's my stepbrother. And maybe that makes me a stepbrother fucker. But you know what? I don't *stepbrotherfucking care*."

I reached my hand out to Mason, and he caught it in his, turning it and kissing my palm, eyes on me. Burning with heat and approval and something else. Something like love.

Because he loved me. And me?

"Because I love him," I told Emily, told the entire arena, told the world. Told Mason, whose eyes went supernova-bright. "We love each other. Legally, our parents are married, but we did nothing wrong. We aren't actually related, and we care about each other. We *choose* each other. And if you can't accept that, if you're still too jealous to let this shit go? Then Emily, I don't know what to tell you, except I don't know. Maybe see a therapist about that."

Lucy giggled. Emily glared at us, opening her mouth and then closing it like a fish. I almost felt sorry for her.

I did feel sorry for her when Mason pulled his jersey off, only to hand it to me.

"Butterfly, you better be wearing my name on your back whenever you're in this building," he told me.

Blushing, but loving how territorial he was, I lifted it over my head. It fell over me, huge and comforting. It smelled just like him—sweat and ocean spray and oranges and danger.

And *mine*. He smelled like mine.

"Sorry I'm late, Mace," I said, a little breathless. "I was working on our presentation."

"Who the fuck cares about our presentation?" He growled, cradling my face with his hands and lowering his lips to mine, kissing me until I couldn't tell whose lips were whose and whose heart was whose and oh, what did it matter anyway, when he held me like this, when we loved each other? What did it matter if he was controlling, manipulative, violent and scary? Yeah, he was my evil stepbrother, but most importantly, he was mine.

Finally, he broke away. "Come on, butterfly. Let's get the fuck out of here."

He lifted me into the air and threw me over his shoulder, skating down the tunnel toward the locker room. I lifted my head, catching something curious: Mason's coach, staring at Lucy like he wanted to swallow her whole.

Oh, shit.

Mason smacked my ass, and I forgot all about it.

31

LESLIE

Once we were alone in the locker room, Mason locked the door before lowering me to the floor, crowding me back against the cubby with his name above it. The room stank of stale sweaty clothes, and I wanted to gag. Instead, I leaned in closer to Mason, surrounding myself with his scent. It should've been gross—he needed a shower—but I could smell the aggression on him, and it made my thighs clench with need.

"Fuck, Leslie," he groaned. "I'll admit, I was ready to tan your pretty little ass for showing up so late, but you made up for it."

"Mason, we can't be here. Your team..."

"They saw us come in here," he said, his lips dropping to my neck. I shivered at the heat and determination in his licks and bites. "They'll give us some time. Daddy needs inside his girl's tight little pussy."

Spinning us around, he walked us backwards, dropping onto a bench and pulling me onto his lap so I straddled him.

He brushed my hair back from my face, staring straight into my eyes.

"You're so beautiful. I've never seen anything so beautiful in my life," he said. And then my heart began to thud because his lips descended toward mine. Just a brush, at first, nothing more than butterfly wings—like he was trying to imitate his nickname for me. The barely there touch of his mouth to mine shouldn't have done anything for me, but my heart felt too big for my chest. Very gently, and so, so slowly, he began to urge my mouth open. It was different from the previous kiss in the stadium; that had been a triumphant conquering, this was a gentle quest. I opened, and his tongue swept in, licking at the corners of my mouth, my tongue, kindling a fire within me. And when he groaned and grabbed the back of my neck so he could force his kiss deeper, kissing me deeper, that small fire roared to life.

I moaned into his mouth, grinding against his hard cock.

He pulled back. "Shh, butterfly. There's no rush."

"But your team," I protested.

He cut me off, kissing me again. It was like the room shifted and shimmered around us. We were somewhere new, somewhere I didn't recognize, and I had no choice but to hold tight to Mason or risk being swept away by the current of his kiss. He slowly lowered me onto the bench, still kissing me. My body felt weak, but my heart had never felt so strong.

Once he'd reduced me to a quivering, emotionally vulnerable mess, he pulled back, his fingers on his lips. I copied him. I could still feel his lips on mine.

"Fuck," he said.

"Uh huh," I gasped.

"I love you, butterfly. You're stuck with me, you hear me?" he said between kisses. "I won't let anything hurt you, all I ask is you stay by my side, alright? Can you promise me that, that you'll stick around no matter how upset our parents are or what people say?"

Could I?

"I'm scared," I admitted, like I had before.

"Fucking terrified," he agreed.

"What if your dad and my mom disown us? What if they can't get their heads around it? What if people talk crap about us, and we have to move, and like, what if our kids—"

Mason interrupted me. "Our kids?"

Uh oh. Too soon? "You don't want kids?" I asked carefully.

"Baby, half the reason why I always come in you without a condom is because I plan to breed your little ass. When it's time, Daddy's going to fuck his babies into you, don't doubt it for a goddamned second. And you're going to take his come like a good girl every time, aren't you? Until you're all round and gorgeous and swollen with my child. Fuck, I cannot wait."

I looked at him warily. "We're freshmen in college."

He sighed. "Fine, I can be convinced to wait a few years. If you're a good girl, that is."

The threat shouldn't have done anything for me, but I went wet, hot, pliant. "I'll be your good girl," I said, lifting my face to his for another kiss. "But what are we going to do when people talk shit about them, Mason? When people point and stare and—"

"Stop. Stop it." He picked me up and deposited me on the bench, kissing each of my wrists gently before lifting them over my head, restraining me against the wood. "Don't get caught up in the what ifs or the shoulds. Here's what's important: I love you, and you love me. I'll protect our kids, just like I protect you."

"Like we protect each other," I corrected.

His eyes warmed as he began to strip me. “Whatever comes, okay?”

I sighed, my heart so full. “Whatever comes.”

“Good. Let me show you who’s coming next. Spoiler alert: It’s you.”

I giggled. “That’s so cheesy.”

He cut off my laugh with another deep, wet kiss, before moving his way down my now naked body, lavishing it with kisses, paying special attention to my breasts, sucking my nipples, tickling my ribs with his lips and making me inhale with pleasure when he licked a circle around my navel and bit both of my hip bones.

“Keep your hands where I put them,” he ordered, and once he was satisfied I’d obey him, he released my wrists. I trembled, forcing them to stay spread behind my head on the bench, as he used his hands to push my thighs apart. Then his mouth was there, licking, and biting my lips, licking up the wetness from my slit, and sucking my clit into his mouth. He worked it with his tongue and I cried out as my core tightened and need wound tighter and tighter.

“Shh. You’ll have to be quiet,” he told me. “My teammates and coach are probably outside, and if any of them hear you, I’ll have to kick their asses and then I’ll be kicked off the team. Can you be quiet, butterfly?”

“I don’t know,” I said, my voice trembling.

In response, he reached up and covered my mouth with his big hand. And then without any preamble, he bit my clit, hard. I came immediately, and the humiliation of him shutting me up that way made the orgasm last.

“One more,” he told me. “And then it’s Daddy’s fat cock’s turn.”

He went back to the beginning, licking and biting at me, swallowing the wetness from inside of me, sucking on my clit and licking circles around it, until I was writhing on the bench. This time when he bit my clit, he kept it between his teeth, making me shriek into his hand, and scream even harder when he released it.

When I'd finally come down, he flipped me over, positioning my hips with my ass in the air and shoving directly into me, once again without any warning. He pumped his hips, using my hair as reins to direct me backwards so he could get the angle right, delivering slaps to my ass as he thrust. The angle was perfect, making it so he hit my g-spot with the crown of his cock every time, and I began winding tight again, feeling another orgasm coming along hard and fast. I wanted to bite down on the wooden bench so no one could hear me moan, but Mason was holding my hair too tight.

Then he released my head, carefully turning it and, with a hand on my neck, pushed my cheek against the solid wood, before spreading my ass cheeks with his thumbs.

"God, I can see both your pretty little holes," he groaned. "The one taking Daddy's cock so well, and the one that's waiting for him to master it."

I jolted underneath him, and he rubbed my back in reassurance.

"Don't worry, butterfly. I'll go slow."

He pumped into me two more times, hitting my G spot each time, and then, just as I was about to come, he pulled out, chuckling as I whined.

"Were you close, butterfly? Don't worry, I've got a better treat in store for you."

With that, he left me on the bench.

And someone began to pound on the door.

32

MASON

She loved me.

She'd told me she loved me. She'd told *everyone* she loved me.

We were going to be together.

And now I was going to cement our relationship with anal—and an engagement ring.

I rifled through my hockey bag, grabbing lube, an unused bullet vibrator I'd bought specifically for Leslie, and the ring box. I'd been a Boy Scout, and I believed in always being prepared. Carefully removing the ring from the box, I hid it in one hand, returning to the bench with the vibe and lube in my other.

One of my teammates was pounding on the door.

Whatever. They could wait.

I dropped everything on the bench, and in order to make sure she was too distracted to see, I turned on the bullet vibe to its highest setting and placed it on her already-sensitive clit. This time, she did scream. Oh, well. If I found out someone heard, I guess I'd have to kill them. Getting kicked off the team was a small sacrifice for hearing her perfect sounds.

As she writhed on the bench, I popped open the cap on the bottle of lube and poured some directly between her ass cheeks and more on my fingers. I began rimming her in small circles. She was panting as the vibe went at her. As she stiffened, I knew she was about to come.

"Butterfly, be a good girl for Daddy and don't come yet," I crooned to her, and she mumbled something incoherent but followed my order.

Slowly, I pushed one finger into her, my poor cock stiffening at the tight feeling as her ass opened and widened for me. Pulling out, I slowly pushed two fingers in this time, then scissored them to stretch her out for my cock.

"You're going to squeeze the hell out of Daddy's fat cock like a good little slut, aren't you, butterfly? Gonna make a home for him inside this virgin hole?"

She moaned at my words.

I pulled my fingers out, delighted to see her dark little hole open up for me for a moment before closing again, like it was winking at me. Lathering my cock up with lube to make it easier for her, I lined myself up.

"Bare down, baby," I told her. "It'll be easier that way."

The pounding got louder.

"Go the fuck away!" I yelled. "I'm busy."

Leslie's entire body flushed red, but she moaned, and I knew the moderate exhibitionism was getting to her. I adored my butterfly's secret kinks.

"You're a fucking asshole!" Matt yelled back, but then it was quiet.

That handled, I started pushing inside her, careful not to go too quickly. A little bit of pain would go a long way—too much and she'd never want to do this with me again.

Fuck, she was so tight. I thought her pussy had been tight, but it had nothing on this.

"Hurts," she moaned.

"I know, baby, I'll go slower."

"No. Hurts not to come," she clarified on a gasp. "Please, M—"

"Please, who?" My voice was like gravel as her ass swallowed my cock, encasing it in its tight heat.

"Please, Daddy. Please let me come."

"Uh uh, butterfly," I scolded. "It's not time yet."

Tell that to my balls. They were heavy as rocks and twice as large by this point. The second she started clenching, I'd be done.

She whined at my words. Worried that she couldn't—or wouldn't—hold off, I reached underneath her and turned off the vibe.

"Noooooo," she cried.

"Yes," I informed her, pulling out and thrusting deeper until I was finally buried all the way in her ass.

"You good, good girl," I said wonderingly. "You've taken all of me. You're such a good girl for Daddy, aren't you? No wonder why I love you."

"I'd love you, too, asshole, if you'd let me come," she complained.

"What did you call me? Words like that won't get you what you want," I warned, trying not to laugh.

As punishment, I didn't give her back the vibe, instead thrusting in and out of her ass faster as my balls began to boil with the need to come.

She was full on crying now, and I imagined that if I could see her poor pussy, it would be a bright, angry red from teasing and neglect.

"Maybe I won't let you come at all," I said conversationally. "You weren't very nice just now."

"No, please, Daddy, please, I need to come again. Let me come."

"And what will you give Daddy for it, huh?"

"Anything. Anything."

There we go. Pushing as deep in her as I could go, I grabbed the ring and reached for her left hand.

It took a little maneuvering—I only had two hands, after all—but I managed to hold her wrist with one hand and slip the ring on her finger with the other.

She gasped.

"Is that what—"

I twisted my hand back underneath her and turned the bullet vibe back on.

"Marry me, butterfly."

Replacing my hands over hers, I laced our fingers together and held her down. I began to thrust again as I spoke. "I know we're young. I know we have a difficult path ahead of us. But I can't see my life without you—haven't been able to since I saw you spinning on the dance floor at our parents' wedding. I'm not a good man, but I'll be the best man I can be for you. I promise." Heart in my throat, I asked, "So butterfly, what do you—"

"Yes!" she cried out, in orgasm, her ass beginning to clench around my cock.

It counted, didn't it?

Just to make sure, I asked, "Yes you'll marry me?"

"Yes, I'll marry you, Daddy. Yes, yes, yes!"

Fuck, yes.

I hammered my hips into her as she squeezed around me, and came, came, came.

"Daddy's coming," I told her in a growl. "Daddy's gonna fill his wife's little ass up with his come."

And then I did, releasing what felt like buckets of come into her ass before I finally collapsed on her in satisfaction.

Not wanting to crush her, I pulled out—and could've come again as my come leaked out of her ass. I loved how sloppy I had made her.

I pulled her—my almost wife—into my arms.

"Did you mean it?" I demanded.

She was breathing heavy.

"No," she told me. Before I could growl in outrage and punish her ass for it, she began laughing, a little breathlessly. "Yes of course I did, you idiot. I love you, and I'll marry you, even though we're way too young."

"Hey, maybe that'll be the bigger issue for your mom," I said, and she started laughing.

"We can only hope."

The pounding started back up.

"Calloway, if you don't unlock this fucking thing, you're off the team," Coach warned through the door.

Ah, fuck.

Making sure Leslie was all covered up in my jersey, I went to unlock the door. Face to face with Coach, I grinned.

"Sorry, Coach. I was busy."

He shook his head. "Get your girlfriend out of my locker room."

"Fiancée," I corrected. "And all due respect, but eyes off of her."

His own eyes narrowed, then he chuckled. "You're a fucking idiot, but you played a good game today, so I don't give a shit about your private life." Spotting Leslie, he said, "You, good luck charm, do me a favor and keep Lucy in line. You do that, I'll pretend this never happened."

I raised an eyebrow, but Leslie shook her head at me, eyes wide.

Whatever. Not my fucking problem. Everything in my life was going according to plan.

Except for one fucking loose end.

33

LESLIE

It was game night.

To be more specific, it was the first hockey game of the season, and I was freaking the hell out. Not because I was worried about how Mason was going to play—even though he was second string, he'd impressed his coach so much over the past couple of weeks. He certainly wouldn't be riding the bench this game.

I sat in the stands, playing with the engagement ring on my finger. It was big but not too big, a cushion cut fire diamond, surrounded by smaller white diamonds. I loved the ring. It was perfect. So I wasn't worried about that, either.

No, the reason why I was worried were the two people walking up the stairs toward me—Mason's father and my mother.

They were here to see Mason play...and, although they didn't know it, for us to tell them we were together.

"Leslie, honey, it's so sweet to see you in your stepbrother's jersey!" my mom said when they reached me. I stood and accepted her hug, trying not to flinch from her words.

Paul caught my eyes over her shoulder. He didn't look like he thought it was sweet. His face was grim.

They sat down next to me, my mother happily chatting away as we watched the players warm up. My eyes tracked Mason as he glided around the rink, stretching his back. As if he could feel me looking, he glanced up into the stands, and grinned.

Hi, butterfly, he mouthed—before he noticed our parents.

He nodded at his father. Once.

His father nodded back. Once.

I resisted hiding my burning face in my hands.

Mason smirked as he went to sit on the bench for the first period. He wasn't starting—yet. But I was so proud of him, and knew it wouldn't be long before he moved up to first string. Before he was leading his team.

"So, Leslie, you two seem to be getting along," Paul remarked.

In the past, I would have hunched, prevaricated, flat out lied. But I'd promised Mason even though we'd tell them together, I wouldn't be ashamed of us. And I wasn't anymore. How could I be, when he loved me so completely, so obsessively, so possessively? And I loved him that way right back?

"We are," I said.

The horn blew, and the game started. I zoned out, barely noticing the team was up by three points, my eyes on Mason's back the entire time.

Until the second period. Tabb was up by six, and Mason rose to his feet, jumping over the board and skating out onto the rink. Suddenly, my eyes were glued to him, to the game. Things moved fast; Mason had the puck, and while I didn't know enough about the game to describe what he was doing, it was like he, his stick, and the puck were one, powerful being. He moved so fast, it was like he was flying.

And then the puck was flying to—right into the net past the opposing team's goalie.

The horn sounded again, and the new score flashed on the scoreboard: 12 Tabb, 3 Cornell.

I jumped to my feet, cheering for Mason.

"Yeah, baby!" I yelled, temporarily forgetting who was with me.

"Baby?" Paul asked.

"Honey, what's that on your hand?" my mom asked, staring in shock at my engagement ring.

Oh, shit.

"An engagement ring, Mom," I said helpfully.

"I know that, honey," she said slowly. "My question is, who the hell *gave* it to you?"

I started to answer, but Mason had just stolen the puck from the other team and was skating toward the net. He passed it to Emory, who passed it to Matt, who then passed it back to Mason—who shot it right into the net. Again.

Jumping up and down wildly, I forgot our parents for a second.

He was incredible. It was like he was dancing.

"Leslie. Answer me." My mom's hand was on mine, tight. "Honey, please."

"Sweetheart, we know the answer," Paul said, his voice as grim as his face.

Shock froze my mother's beautiful face.

"Honey, you—"

But Mason had the puck again, and we watched in silent awe as he scored a hat trick, just as horn sounded to signal the end of the second period.

Mason's team was whooping and hollering. Mason,

however, skated over to our side of the stadium. He pointed at me, then pointed at his father, then pointed at me again.

I held up my ring finger.

He nodded, waiting on the rink.

"Calloway!" his coach called.

"We're together," I told our parents, my voice trembling. I was proud. Scared of their reactions, but proud. "We love each other. I'm not asking for your permission—you know Mason won't care—but I am asking for your acceptance."

"Oh, honey," my mom began.

Paul stood. "I don't know what my son did to you, Leslie, but I promise, I'll make it right."

And then he was making his way down the stands as I watched.

"Calloway!" Mason's coach called again.

Squaring his shoulders, Mason tipped his chin at me. I knew what it meant.

Are you okay?

I nodded.

That was good enough for him. Mason turned, following his team back into the locker room—where, I assumed, his father was going to find him.

34

MASON

There was a man waiting for me outside the locker room.

Surprisingly, it wasn't my father.

Jack Feldman leaned against the wall about a foot away from the locker room door, his eyes trained on me. A few of the players spoke to him as they filed into the locker room, but I couldn't hear what they said. Probably fawning all over him. He was a legend, after all.

"Nice hat trick," he commented when he saw me. "Although you're going to have to pick up your speed when you play Reina, or I'm going to be bored out of my mind."

"Why are you here, Jack?" I asked, scanning the hallway for my father.

"Wanted to make sure that Vixen went to good use, and I didn't have to call my brother for a clean-up. But I saw the ring on her finger. Pretty girl. Nice work."

I stilled. "You'll keep your eyes to yourself if you know what's good for you."

The bastard chuckled. "Don't worry, I have my eyes on my own prize." He stood, holding out a hand to shake mine.

I accepted the handshake—and the way he squeezed my hand like he was trying to grind the bones together.

"But Mason, I find out you or any of the fuckers on your team are using Vixen more...recreationally? I promise you, there's nowhere any of you can run to where I won't find you."

I considered this, then leaned in. "What if I told you there was a certain RA, who, if he got his hands on Vixen, would probably use it 'recreationally.'"

Did I know for sure Chris would try to roofie a girl with it? No. Did I have a hunch? Yes. Did I care if I was wrong? Definitely no.

I'd have to tell Leslie. She'd be pissed. Ah, well.

Jack released my hand, but watched me, like he was reading my mind.

"Name?"

I gave him Chris' last name.

He smirked. "Thanks for the intel. Good luck."

Without glancing back at me, he made his way down the hallway and disappeared out of sight.

Which was when my father appeared.

"Dad," I said.

"Son, explain what the hell you think you're doing."

I glanced at the clock in the corner. Only eight minutes until third period.

"Are you playing a game?"

"Hopefully."

He glared at me. "You know what I mean, Mason."

"I'm not playing with Leslie, Dad. I'm dead serious about her. I'm marrying her. And you aren't fucking getting in our way."

He pinched the bridge of his nose. "This is a shitty way to rebel and punish me for remarrying."

Fucking hell.

"It's not about you, Dad!" I exploded. "It hasn't been about you for years—you made that easy. Leslie is the first good thing I've had since Mom died. I accept that you found someone new to love. I accept that you're happy now. Can't you accept the same from me?"

He started to speak, but I raised my hand. "No. It's important to Leslie that you and her mom give us your blessing or whatever, but it's not important to me. I'm not giving her up for anything, and if you try to make me, I'll take her somewhere far away."

My dad raised an eyebrow. "And Leslie would be okay with that?"

I sighed. "Probably not, but I wouldn't give her the option."

My dad shut his eyes, sighing. "That sounds healthy."

"It works for us," I said. "You don't have to like it. It's how it is."

My dad finally opened his eyes, watching me. "It's important to me that you're happy. That she's happy. If this makes you both happy..."

"It does."

"Then I'll learn to accept it," he said.

My shoulders released, tension I hadn't realized I'd been holding flowing out of me. I hadn't been lying when I said that if he tried to get in between us, I'd take Leslie far away. But it would make her unhappy, and that was unacceptable.

"Thank you," I said.

My father looked up at the clock. "You only have a few minutes, you should go talk to your team. But Mason?"

"Yeah?"

"Nice work out there."

It was the closest he'd get to telling me he was proud of

me. In the past, I wouldn't have let it affect me, but Leslie had softened me up like a teddy bear, and so I felt the praise, and I'd be lying if it didn't make me glow, just a little.

That glow grew when our goalie shut out Cornell from scoring, and we beat them, 15 to 3—and I scored the final goal.

And it turned into a supernova when Leslie forgot herself and ran out onto the ice after the game and jumped into my arms.

I skated around in circles with her long legs wrapped around my hips, not caring who was watching.

"You were amazing," she said excitedly.

"Did you have any idea what was happening?" I teased.

She shook her head, hair flying every which way. "No freaking idea. Sportspuckball, you know."

I laughed. "I need to teach you hockey."

She kissed me, giggling. "I love when you teach me things."

I stared into her dark eyes, feeling like I could conquer the world. And I would conquer the world, with her at my side.

She was the most beautiful woman I'd seen in my entire life.

And I loved her more than I loved anything.

"Oh, butterfly," I said. "We're just getting started."

THE END

Want more Mason? **Read the bonus epilogue here.**

Hockey king and resident sociopath, Jack Feldman, is getting his own book! **Puck It** ***is coming soon...*** *You can sign up for my newsletter for updates.*

Want to get to know Jack's older, even more sociopathic brother? ***If you're reading the ebook, flip the page for a preview*** *of* Bad Heroes — *my dark why choose trilogy about three rogue ex-Navy SEALs and the woman who got away...but not for long. ;)*

Finally: An author's career is made by reviews from readers. So if you enjoyed *Butterfly*, could you pretty please go give it a review on Amazon? I'd be so fucking grateful. Thank you!

ALSO BY JO BRENNER

Bad Heroes

You Can Follow Me

Lose Me In The Shadows

Meet Me In The Dark

ACKNOWLEDGMENTS

First, thank you to Brittney and Jen, who didn't laugh me off the face of the planet when I said, *I want to write a dark romance novella called* My Stepbrother Daddy. No, you both are true friends, because you helped me brainstorm possible new pen names for the project...even though I ended up writing it under this one.

Sabrina, thank you for reading this book in its earliest, most dire straits, and helping me glean out the character and story mixed in among the filthy sex. And for always being on the other end of the phone when I need you. I love you.

Jasmine, as always, thank you for keeping me sane. And for alpha-ing this one, and helping me make sure that Mason was daddy-ing enough.

Thank you to my editor, Surey: If it weren't for you, this whole story would be a complete mess.

Thank you so much to my beta readers—Tori, Jennifer, Newt, Adrienne, and Jeramie—who picked up the draft, devoured it in a few days, and provided such helpful feedback. I hope I did you proud.

Thank you so much to my ARC readers, who agreed to take the time to read another filthy little book from me. Or take a chance on me for the first time. Y'all are champions, and deserve the best of everything.

And to my street team: I love you all. I would also give

you the shirt off my back, but barring that, I am getting you all shirts. <3

Conor's Good Girls: Your support, on Patreon and beyond, has made my week, my month, my year. Thank you.

Poppy, thank you for doing what you always do—finding the holes and helping me fill them. (Yes, that *is* what she said.) And for being such a great fucking collaborator and friend.

Kenya, I've becoming so reliant on our TikTok Live writing sprints, I can't write without you now. So you better get online, friend.

Thank you to Terry and Sierra, who helped me think through the whole "so I wrote a novella, now what do I do with it?" thing. I don't know what I would do without the two of you. Probably cry in a corner a lot.

And finally, to my readers: Thank you, thank you, thank you. Every time you pick up one of my books, my heart grows three sizes. It's gotten pretty damn big (that's *also* what she said), and I'm so very, very grateful.

ABOUT THE AUTHOR

A lover of dogs, mountain adventures, and HGTV, Jo Brenner writes romances that are little bit twisted, a lotta bit sexy—and always have an HEA.

Stay in touch and get the latest publishing updates, book teasers, book recommendations, and more by joining her Facebook readers' group, Jo Brenner's Bar, and by subscribing to her newsletter!

facebook.com/AuthorJoBrenner
x.com/jo_brenner
instagram.com/jobrennerbooks
tiktok.com/@jobrennerbooks
goodreads.com/Jo_Brenner
amazon.com/author/Jo_Brenner
bookbub.com/profile/jo-brenner

Made in United States
Orlando, FL
03 September 2024

51096295R00157